REQUIEM FOR
PARISH

A SUPERNATURAL MYSTERY

DOUGLAS COCKELL

For Bob and Val

With special thanks to Dylan Cockell for
his generous ideas and story-telling skills,
and thanks to Fred Oliver and John Bridgeman
for showing me their inspiring house.

Copyright © 2024 Dunhill Clare Publishing

Requiem For Parish

A Supernatural Mystery

By Douglas Cockell

First Edition

dunhillclare@gmail.com

Edited by Jody Freeman

Published in Ontario, Canada

Hardcover ISBN: 978-1-990469-69-5

Paperback ISBN: 978-1-990469-70-1

Ebook   ISBN: 978-1-990469-71-8

Library and Archives Canada Cataloguing in Publications

Requiem For Parish is the fourth book in the Requiem Series.

The previous series titles are:

Requiem For Thursday (Book 1)

Requiem For Noah (Book 2)

Requiem For Mary Mac (Book 3)

PROLOGUE

Under one focussed light the woman's naked body is bright against the green linens and plastic sheeting. The rest of the operating room is a circle of looming shadows—but the surrounding darkness is important, too.

The ghosts need room to appear, assemble, and withdraw. They draw on the colourless shadows to muster and form. They need the gloom behind the darkened monitors and x-ray armatures, the anaesthetic array and the wheeled trays of instruments. That's where they take on substance, congealing from the air to timidly approach the table.

The Archer knows he can only afford the one overhead light to work by, knowing he needs the shadows as much as he needs the light.

He imagines the ghosts are afraid of his waking world, afraid that if they come too close, they'll become flesh again and succumb to the scarcely remembered drag of passing time, as though they were stepping from a peaceful rest back up onto a gaudy, noisy carousel. They've been beyond all that tedious motion, out of the creaking clockwork of time, and now here *he* is, this chunky, broad-shouldered man, calling out to them so that even out there in the deepest pool of oblivion, out on the wandering plane, they are forced to take notice of him. Drawn by a compulsion almost like curiosity, a few of them assemble in the gloom—assemble in numbers and assemble in form.

They listen to him drone on, hour after hour: "Anima eius, et animae omnium fidelium defunctorum…"

It seems to the square-shouldered man that there is a silent crowd in the shadows. Some of the shades peer at the woman's body on the operating table, and some part of their awareness remembers compassion. And so, they drift away in horror, repulsed, back across the umbral, back into the tranquil and painless nothingness from which they came.

There are others, though. Others who feel an old and vile excitement as they become aware of the woman's nakedness. They linger and leer, and then, only grudgingly, do they fade back as others with a greater claim to this place and this moment in time edge forward.

But it's a woman The Archer wants, a woman at once remembered, loved, and hated. That's why he conjures with these strange words and this naked woman here and now—this newly departed soul of a wife and mother—as she lies on the operating table, her body still warm.

If he keeps calling out, keeps sacrificing, eventually, she will have to come back to him, stepping forward, drawn back into the light.

CHAPTER ONE

Carly Rouhl, majority owner and former editor of *Escarpment Magazine*, was walking with her friend Harriet Blaine along the south side of Lakeshore Road. Carly's Lab, Indy, was on a leash with a gizmo that could be released and coiled back in with a button. Indy didn't seem to be taking all that flexibility well, trying to race ahead, getting in the way of pedestrians, and then bouncing back against her leg.

Carly and Harriet couldn't see much of the adjacent park and lake because of the bushes and trees at street level, and the cars flowed in a constant susurration on the roadside.

Harriet took Carly's arm and tugged. Carly looked at her in surprise. As usual, Harriet's face was open and guileless, pretty in a child-like way, her large glasses making her green eyes appear even larger. She seemed an odd choice for the magazine's new editor, but Carly had seen the relentless efficiency behind her friend's appearance.

"What's going on?" Carly asked as Harriet steered towards a set of stone steps leading down into the park.

Harriet wiped blond hair off her brow where it was clinging

to a smear of sunblock. "It's obvious to me that you've got something on your mind. I think we should talk."

"We were talking."

"But this looks serious to me. We need shade and a bench."

Indy, tired of the hot sidewalk, sensed that things were looking up and led the way to the steps.

Carly allowed herself to be led down into the lakeside park, grateful for the shade of a massive willow tree. She raised her sunglasses to her head. "The Naval Memorial? I haven't been down here in a while."

Harriet sat relaxed against the arm of a bench and closed an eye. "Now, what's bothering you? Are you and Evan okay?"

Carly frowned at her for a moment, then sagged against the bench and sighed. She pressed the button on Indy's leash, and, with a purring sound, the Lab dragged the leash out to its full length.

"Evan?" She groaned. "What can I say? I'm sleeping with a celebrity. He's so slick he drives me nuts. I think it's good that we only spend weekends together."

"Is he being a jerk about it? Being a TV star and all?"

"Nah. He's too perfect for that. The big hunk loves me, for God's sake. Go figure."

"So...?"

"Well, you know—he's a trained researcher, and yet there he is on a Lunch Date show, smiling at some himbo, asking him when his new track drops."

"Himbo?"

"Male bimbo. Try to keep up." She made a sort of genteel sniff. "No, it's not Evan. The poor guy. I give him such a hard time about being a talk show host, but he's doing fine. We're... okay, I guess."

"It's not the magazine, I hope."

"Of course not. You're doing a great job running things."

"So, why do you keep showing up, sitting at your old desk? The staff still look to you for direction, you know. You've been there three times this week and all you do is sit there with your laptop."

"Oh, God! I don't mean to undercut your authority, Harriet. You're the editor now. I just... I'm having a little trouble with my new life."

"Being a writer, you mean?"

"Being a fiction writer, I guess. When I'm at home with my laptop—alone—I sort of stare at my screen and... Well, I imagine things."

"That's what all story writers do."

"I know. This is silly, but lately, I've been afraid."

"Afraid?"

"I've told you everything, Harriet. About these last few months...You know what happens when I let my imagination go. You saw how I got with that little Dora girl. It was as if I saw that poor dead child, alive in a schoolroom that hasn't existed in a century. The reality is she was long dead. I even saw an old photograph of her corpse, propped up with her parents at her side. They used to do that, you know."

"I remember. You've had experiences. Unsettling experiences."

"Experiences? Is that what we're calling them now? I'm starting to wonder if it's in my genes. Dad used to go all dreamy and zone out when he was writing. Of course, he was drinking back then—back when he was writing his best stuff, the books he's famous for. But that wasn't it. It wasn't the alcohol. He was in a...state. I can't describe it, but it was where his best work came from."

Carly rubbed her eyebrow. "The other day, I was staring into the shop front at Modella's and there was this moment: I'm standing there in the heat, squinting at the glare off the shop window, and it's like there was a spark behind me and the sudden smell of burning skin. A shock went through me, and I staggered—right there with people walking by."

"My God. Have you seen a doctor?"

Carly closed her eyes and shook her head. "I felt all right afterwards, at least when my breathing slowed. I stood there on the sidewalk, stupidly trying not to attract any more attention as people shuffled by. The experience just came and went, but the bizarre part is, I somehow *knew* what had happened. I understood it as though I witnessed the very act."

"Act? What act?"

"A woman was struck on the back of the neck with one of those shock things. You know, a taser? I even felt her collapse. I knew it because I saw it—and felt it! Someone wanted to kill the poor woman. Maybe...maybe he did."

There was stunned silence, then Harriet's expression softened, and she touched Carly's hand. "You're thinking it's like with the schoolhouse and the little girl; when you felt you were actually there with her. You had a vision."

Carly gave a bitter laugh. "There's a name for that kind of experience; they call it dissociation. For a split second, you lose control. You're outside yourself. But I can't help wondering, is that how schizophrenia begins?" She rested her brow on her hand. "You know, when you're writing stories the way I do now, you kind of have to let go sometimes, and when I do that, it's like I get a little lost—somewhere between reality and the mind's eye. I'm afraid of where this is taking me."

Harriet's eyes darted, not knowing how to offer comfort. At last, she said, "Everyone knows your dad was a genius, a towering literary figure. He had that uncanny intuition. Was he ever...unstable?"

Carly's frown softened. There was no point taking offence. The one undeniable fact of Carly's life was that she lived in the shadow of a great man. It touched everything she did and loomed over everything she had accomplished.

"His generation of writers were hard living," she said. "But nothing clinical. His suicide was a choice and—given his state of health—not a crazy one. On the other hand, he was a country mile away from normal. That was his genius, of course, but what about me? I can't use the excuse of genius."

"Give it time."

Carly laughed. "Anyway, thanks for taking the magazine off my shoulders. One less strain on my fragile mind." Her gaze ranged out over the park at the mothers and their children playing around the memorial. "I mean, look at all these people, enjoying the sunshine in their shorts and halter tops, and here am I obsessing about a doorway."

Harriet blinked in confusion. "What's this? Something new?"

Carly shot a glance sideways at her. "Kind of." She hunched her shoulders and went on playing Indy like a fish. "I was sitting with Indy in the living room last night when he suddenly perked up and looked down the hallway to my father's old office. I spoke to Indy—you know, tried to calm him, but off he trotted down the hall and began sniffing at the door to the office. I followed, wondering what he was reacting to. There was no sound, and the door was firmly shut the way it always is, but he was doing that thing with his head, cocking it this way and that. Indy was my father's dog, you know. The way he was behaving kind of freaked me out, but I'm a rational person; despite all the stuff that's happened to me over the last couple of years, I refuse to be afraid of anything. So, I went to open the door. I mean, what would you have done?" Carly paused. "And it wouldn't open."

"It was locked?"

"That door is never locked. The knob turned, but the door was jammed shut. That happened to me once before."

"When your father died."

"Do you remember what I told you? I had shut off the heat in the house after they took away his body. I was staying in my condo then, so I figured, why heat the place, right? But that door—the door to his office… When I came to check on the place, that one door was warm. The door was *warm!* Swollen in its frame, you see."

"But you got in."

"Yeah, I put my shoulder to it, and it swung free."

"And the office was empty?"

"Of course it was. Dad was gone. Death by suicide—shot himself. It's been over a year since then. I've had a year of being alone in life."

"You have Evan."

"Now I do. Back then, when Dad died, Evan was… I had driven him away. We weren't really together."

"So, wait. You're saying the door jammed again? And this was…?"

"Just last night. And there's no reason for it to do that. The whole house is warm now."

"Well, it could be the humidity making it expand and contract. So, what? You forced the door open again?"

"That's what I would have done. That's what the sane, rational Carly would have done. It's what I did back then. This time? This time I was afraid—not of my father's ghost or any of that nonsense. I was afraid I was losing it. Losing control. You see what I mean? It's the same worry."

"What did you do?"

"I just left Indy staring at the door, and I went back to my chair in the living room. This morning, the door opened normally, and nothing was disturbed, as I knew it would be."

"You've always rejected the idea that you're…you know, psychic."

Carly laughed. "I've read those stories, the ones where the heroine has some sort of psychic gift, and I've always thought they're nuts. A woman like that? She'd be scared shitless all the time, or she'd be certifiably insane." She slapped a hand on her knee. "You either live in this world with its rules, or you're an outcast. All those witches you read about down through history —by the standards of our time, they were psychotic, not psychic. I feel for them; it must have been real easy to go crazy back then, but I'm not going down that particular path, thank you very much."

"Yet you're afraid?"

Carly fixed Harriet with a look that was filled with a nameless anxiety. "Yeah. I'm afraid that I'm losing my way."

Harriet brushed Carly's hand with her own. For a split second, Carly felt the need to pull away. She was acutely aware that her friend once yearned for her as a lover. Maybe she still did. What would it be like, Carly wondered, to be worthy of all that love? Instead, she grasped Harriet's hand like the child Carly felt herself to be.

"You're spending too much time alone in your father's house," Harriet said. "Move in with Evan and start a new life. Maybe you could deed the Rouhl house to the city; they've been wanting to make it a historic site. You could afford it with your dad's royalties."

Indy took off towards the steps, chasing something they couldn't see, which swept his leash across a wide swath of grass. Carly leapt up to avoid tangling innocent civilians in Indy's wake, and the conversation ended in a scramble.

It's too bad. If Carly had stayed, looked to her right, and followed the curve of the

distant beach strip, she might have been able to make out a lakeside home, one among many stretching down towards Hamilton.

Maybe, in the quantum haze of time and space, she would have sensed a connection with the woman living there.

Or perhaps, letting go, she would have discerned the "particular path" skirting the shore where her fears were leading her.

CHAPTER TWO

It struck him immediately that it would make the perfect coffin. The mattress came in a cardboard box only five feet by two. Inside the box, the mattress was shrink-wrapped into a tight cylinder. Once taken out of the box and the plastic cut with scissors, the mattress unrolled itself and began to expand. Right before your eyes, it puffed up to a full-size mattress perfect for his bed. It was like magic.

By a kind of twisted logic that even he didn't understand, the press called him "The Archer" and right now, dark-eyed and heavy-set, he was wheeling the box along a corridor on an upright baggage cart. It was an industrial-quality hand cart made of tubular steel, easily available on-site in one of the storage rooms.

The cart made a slight rhythmic squeak as it rolled over the floor, which bothered him. Not that there was anyone around to take notice. The reception hall, nurses' station, the wide staircase, elevator banks, and the examination rooms were all empty. IV stands were pushed against the walls along with the gurneys and blood pressure monitors. It was just that the relentless squeaking seemed to take away from the solemnity of the occasion.

After all, not more than six hours ago, the woman in the cardboard box had been full of laughter and excitement. Her eyes, wide with anticipation, were still fresh in his mind.

He wheeled his load past the deserted nurses' station, the mattress box mounted vertically on the cart. He always bent their knees and bowed their heads to make them fit. The dead body itself didn't interest him except as a challenge to dispose of.

There were advertising designs printed playfully all along the sides of the cardboard box, promising a peaceful night's sleep on the nation's best-selling mattress. The design included blue teddy bears and sheep jumping fences. He remembered that the inside surfaces of the box were printed with a cloud design, which he thought was a nice touch.

The Archer also remembered the first time he had opened the box. It made him chuckle to think no one would imagine such a thing as a mattress could fit inside that compact box. Just as no one would imagine what he had in there now.

Of course, he could have used one of the four-wheeled gurneys pushed against the walls to wheel the corpse out to his car. They were rubber-tired and easy to manoeuvre, but it would have looked strange when he rolled his load out into the parking lot. There might be someone driving by this time of night, and the parking lot was well lit for security reasons.

He passed two consulting rooms and a waiting area. The waiting room was quite pleasant. There were floor-to-ceiling windows along one wall and through these windows, he could see the streets of New Orleans and the dark curve of the Missis-sippi between two and three-story buildings fronted with balconies and wrought iron railings. He couldn't see the parking lot through the windows, of course, which made sense, but it seemed odd nevertheless because he knew the lot was right there.

He was almost at the exit door, a short roll past rows of chrome clothing racks, each holding a dozen gowns, suits, and medical scrubs. Then he was in the small double door entrance-way. This was the hardest part—getting the cart over the slight bump of the weatherproof doors. The doors were reinforced glass but heavily framed and mounted. He had to use his shoulder to hold the door open and turn the cart so that he could pull it over the threshold sash out onto the tarmac.

The rest was easy. His Toyota Highlander hybrid was parked conveniently close, and—as if to bless the whole enterprise—there was a parking sign near the door with his actual name on it. How perfect it all was! How apt!

He opened the trunk with his key fob and waited while the tailgate rose, then he wiggled the box off the tongue of the cart so that it was sitting on the warm asphalt of the parking lot. The big empty lot still radiated heat off into the night. He tilted the box so that it fell against his trunk, and he bent over to take the lower end in both hands. Some considerate designer had provided an oval hand hole in each end of the box to make it easier to handle, so he could get a good grip and lift. His finger-tips pressed against the plastic wrap inside the box, and he fancied that he could feel the woman's toes. He remembered how red her nails were—almost the same colour as his wife's.

The heavy box tipped easily into the trunk and slid over the vinyl liner. The back seats were down, so the cardboard coffin fitted almost as well as it would have in a hearse. He touched the tailgate, and it began to swing down slowly until it clicked shut. He locked the car, just to be safe, and dragged the empty cart back towards the entryway.

Using his keycard, he opened the outer door and began the long, quiet walk back to the storage room. The rhythmic squeak of the hand cart didn't echo. There was too much drapery, privacy screens, bulletin boards, and plush benches for that.

He made a right turn past the OR and used his card again to get into the storage area. It was dark inside where the faint security lights couldn't reach, but his phone was all the light he would need. Taking care to make sure the cart was where he'd found it, he closed up and walked back the way he had come.

The rest of the parking lot was entirely empty, so he put his SUV into a wide circling turn towards the road exit. Always careful, he took a second to look both ways before pulling out onto the service road. The night was dark and moonless, but there were light standards at regular intervals along the wide loop of the industrial estate.

He passed a big building that housed The Weather Network and another that printed massive vinyl sheets for billboards. In all the driveways and parking lots of the industrial area, he never passed a car. Plenty of silent trucks and trailers but not a living soul.

In a few short minutes, he was on the highway, and there was still a bit of traffic here, even as late as this. He took the longer route up through Dundas and on up the scenic road above the escarpment. That took him past farmland to the semi-rural road leading into Waterdown. He watched for the cutoff and ground over gravel for a few minutes until he was at the lip of a lighted quarry.

Choosing a dark strip between two light poles, he unloaded the cardboard box, being careful not to crush the corners on the ground. With the box on its end, he tipped it just enough to let him open the box lid. A clear plastic bag tumbled out, raising a little dust.

Alternately rolling and tugging at the bag, he managed to expose Carmen's body: a middle-aged, dark-haired woman on the shadowed gravel. Standing over her reverently, he mumbled a prayer and crossed himself, then he used his foot to roll her off the plastic sheeting and over the slope. There was a cascade of loose stones and a puff of grey dust…and then silence.

He folded the plastic bag and stuffed it into the box; he would be needing them both again.

CHAPTER THREE

It was the second time the girl had just shown up in Lizzie's living room. Like before, she stood there on the basement steps and moved her lips without a sound escaping them. She appeared to be in her late teens, pretty, with the casual primness of a churchgoer. After no more than three minutes, the girl disappeared again.

Lizzie Collier, slender, round-shouldered, and grey, stepped around to the stairwell and took a wary step down after her. At least this time, Lizzie was sure the girl had gone down to her basement. She'd seen her go down—and there hadn't been an exit from the basement level since they took the railway line away in the late fifties. That meant the girl was still down there, didn't it?

Careful not to take her eyes off the basement stairs, she turned, went back up, and got her phone from the end table by the couch. For the second time in a week, Lizzie poked in 911. Then she sat on the couch and waited for the police to make a second visit. This time, they came at around two on a hot afternoon.

The first time she had called 911, it had been close to eleven in the morning, and the police hadn't taken Lizzie's intruder too seriously. A couple of uniformed police had come to her door less than ten minutes after that first phone call. They came in and did a quick search of her house, upstairs and down, but they didn't find anybody. Maybe this time, the responding officers would be more receptive.

Lizzie's house on the beach strip was comfortable but odd, full of bric-a-brac that hadn't quite made it to antique status: an old optometrist window sign that served as a lamp stood on a table made of intertwined driftwood branches, the lamp's worn and abraded eye still watchful. Mixed in with the comfortable couch and armchair, scale models of carnival rides and tin gas station signs gave the space a mid-century casual look. Some people called it "Americana" and others "Petrolia" because these were vestiges of the grand era of the American automobile.

And now, here were the police again: two officers in service vests and short sleeve summer uniform shirts walking warily into her living room in answer to her second call. They were different cops from the first time, a young man and an older woman. They took a moment, registering mild surprise at the decorative pieces before doing a search.

Lizzie stood straight and smoothed her pale paisley house-coat, trying to appear rational and composed. "I think the girl must be downstairs; a girl in a blouse and skirt. Dark hair, about five foot four or so."

The woman cop spoke with a slight accent. Eastern European maybe. She pulled out a small tablet and tapped at it for a few seconds. "Mrs. Elizabeth Collier." She raised her eyes from the screen. "The call said the intruder was a teenager. Didn't say a word to you. That right?"

"Well… It looked like she was talking, but I didn't hear a thing."

"Your hearing normal?"

"Yes. I mean, I'm in my seventies now, but I can still hear okay."

The two officers looked at one another, then the woman cop nodded, and they went down to the basement, but it was an informal affair this time—no drawn weapons, no doors slammed aside.

Lizzie noticed and knew, once again, she was being judged. When they finished the search, she followed their eyes to the wall hangings and display case. The young man bent over a perfectly clean ashtray carved to look like a bird bath, complete with two doves, and Lizzie felt the need to explain.

"My husband used to collect things," she said. "It was our business—antiques and collectibles. Americana."

The young male cop nodded. He had a closely buzzed beard trimmed to follow his jawline. "Okay, so we didn't find anyone," he said. "Is anything missing? Damage or disruption anywhere in the house?"

"No, nothing."

"It was a young woman you saw, a girl, and she wasn't holding anything; a bag, a camera maybe?"

"She made me think of a high school senior," Lizzie said. "I used to teach at a community college. I'm good with young people but, of course, I was surprised at her being in my house in the middle of the day. The first time I saw her standing there on the top steps of my basement staircase, I froze."

The woman pulled out the tablet from her shirt pocket and tapped some more. "It's, what, just after two?" She studied the screen. "Your last call was at eleven A.M."

Lizzie nodded, wondering what significance the time might have.

"Those steps, the ones leading down to your basement?" The young man turned his head and nodded at the bannister protecting the stairwell. "That's where she was standing?"

"Both times. Yes. Quite a pretty girl in a modest sort of way, but she seemed…not frightened exactly, but concerned. You know, worried. Maybe she was annoyed at something. I really couldn't read her expression."

"You're sure her lips were moving?"

"She seemed to be talking to *me*, honestly! But I couldn't hear a word she was saying. It was like TV with the sound turned down. I didn't want to make any sudden moves, but this time when it happened, I scarcely blinked and suddenly she was disappearing down the basement steps."

"To the basement? You're sure?"

"Positive. I carefully backed away to the fireplace and picked up my phone. The first time she showed up, I had no idea where she had gone. I went through the whole house, sort of shaking a poker and looking in every room, but I couldn't find her. I didn't check every cupboard and corner, mind you. I was too scared. There's no way I wanted to corner her in the basement, so I didn't go down there at all. But this time, I *definitely* saw her go down to the basement."

The cop scratched his beard. "We looked about down there. Plenty of places to hide among all those crates and boxes, but I'm sure there's no one down there."

"Right. You're saying there's no one in my house but me."

"There's no one here now." His tone was reassuring as though he were speaking to a child. "We were thorough."

There didn't seem to be anything else to say, so Lizzie shrugged. "Would you like a cup of tea?" Her voice, a teacher's voice, was calm and unhurried.

The young man looked at his partner. The fortyish, stocky woman looked androgynous in her blue vest. Lizzie got the impression that the young cop was being given a chance to get experience with people while the older woman observed and took notes.

The female officer nodded slightly to the young man, and he turned back to Lizzie. "Sure. Tea would be nice."

Afterwards, Lizzie got it. There were probably protocols for this sort of thing. The two officers wanted to see if she was a woman in crisis, mentally unstable or senile, so she went about setting out the tea things efficiently and serving gracefully. Lizzie hadn't bothered with makeup that morning, but her housecoat was new and fashionable, and her slippers playfully cute. Her hair was mostly grey but neatly brushed, her long bangs pinned above her right ear.

The two officers sipped tea and made conversation but soon left, satisfied that she wasn't crazy—or so Lizzie hoped.

———

After they had gone up the garden steps and over the bike path, Lizzie took her teacup and sat in the comfortable armchair by the window she favoured. She frowned at the surface of her coffee table and tried to imagine what the police would make of this.

Today, she saw the girl and it was Thursday right after lunch. She'd microwaved a hot dog. This time, she'd made an effort to notice details before she called the police. She knew her credibility would be on the line again.

What on earth was the girl after?

Lizzie sipped her tea and thought. What would a teenager with a longish grey skirt worn with a plain, round collared blouse want with an old widow like her? Had she ever taught the girl? No. Lizzie had been retired five years already. The girl was too young.

And the girl was talking. Yes, definitely talking.

Except this time, Lizzie was absolutely sure there wasn't a sound coming from the girl's mouth; just that sad, stressed look and her lips tight and drawn in anger. In fact, it dawned on Lizzie that the girl seemed to be behaving pretty much the way she had the first time she'd appeared—at eleven on a hot, humid Monday.

Lizzie closed her eyes and tried to remember...

When she was finished talking, the girl stood still, sort of slumped her shoulders, and, with a defeated look, took the steps down to the basement—not hurried but briskly, as though she was exasperated with Lizzie's failure to understand.

That first time, Lizzie had walked up to the railing and looked down. The basement light was on and there was no sign of the girl on the landing. That was interesting. There was a motion sensor light on the lower landing, and the girl's movements must have tripped it on.

Shaking her head, Lizzie went on sipping her tea and allowed herself a slow glance at the stairwell. She wasn't frightened, but she didn't like the idea that she wasn't secure in her own house. After all, it had pretty much become her world these last few years.

CHAPTER FOUR

Deputy Superintendent Filman caught Detective Prem Joshi in the Halton Police Services Three District cafeteria. Filman's uniform looked crisp and pressed; Joshi looked soft and settled, burrowed in a shadowy corner far from the heat of the windows. Not wanting to look too officious, Filman took a minute getting himself a coffee and a cupcake in plastic wrap. When Filman approached, Joshi scraped his chair as though about to rise but Filman waved him down.

With practiced casualness, he said, "How's the quarry thing going?"

Joshi, squat, sallow-faced, heavy-lidded and wary, looked at Filman's cupcake. "We've identified the woman—another mother from the Latino community, name of Carmen, wife of Hal Lenz. It's our killer, all right. Carmen makes three."

"A body dump, of course."

Filman sat and sighed, unwrapping his cupcake; half its height was swirling icing. Filman looked thin and angular, this made more apparent by his height. Joshi tried to hide his jealousy.

"Yeah. Dropped off from a vehicle," Joshi said. "We couldn't get anything from the tire tracks. Too much dust and wind. She was rolled down a gravel embankment. Naked, mutilated, so we figure she was dragged to the edge of the pit and pushed over."

"Maybe the guy's not too strong? Didn't try to pick her up."

Joshi slowly tipped his head from side to side. "She's a bit over average weight, so yeah. Maybe. This guy is not careful, like he either wants to get caught or he's sure of himself. No attempt to cover or hide the body—just wanted rid of it. This time of year, late summer, somebody would have smelled something, even if that landscaper hadn't spotted her down there. Last time, he dumped the body in a karst."

"What's a karst? Wait, is this a setup for a joke?"

"No, no! Let me have my moment. I've been waiting months for someone to ask me what a karst is. It's a vertical split in rocky terrain. There are a few in Hamilton. The point is the body was easily visible to passers-by."

"Still waiting on forensic testing?"

"On the latest, yeah, but it's pretty obvious. It's the same mutilation as the two others: left breast removed. Same as the body discovered back in March in a Hamilton park—Abby. And the one in February left in a snowbank, that was Maria."

"Figures." Filman raised an eyebrow. "You think the mutilation means something? Taking the breast?"

"The mutilation was on the left side, over the heart. Just a speculation, but if it's ritual, that could speak to the killer's intention."

Filman stretched, trying to affect a merely casual interest. "Mm. Ritual. So, some kind of mystical thing, I guess."

Joshi looked up and frowned, sensing that something was up.

"What does the Predpol software tell you?" Filman asked.

"Not much. The computer projection lights up a half-dozen neighbourhoods centred around Lakeshore and Mapleview.

There's an old church nearby that mostly services the Latino community."

Wiping his fingers on a paper napkin, Filman crumpled it, letting it drop like a chestnut on the plastic wrap. "How long have you been on this case?"

"Six months now; since the winter. We're working on the assumption the three murders are by the same psycho."

"The media are tagging the guy as 'The Archer.' Because of the breast thing?"

"Yeah. Don't call him that in front of Eilert, though. He hates the way these things get packaged for the media. Besides, he's apt to remind you that the female Amazon warriors were supposed to remove their *right* breasts so they could pull a bowstring, not the left."

Filman mugged an apology. "Well, *excuse* me. Eilert reads too much. Any headway?"

"All three women were Latinas, dark-haired, active Catholics. Probably not chosen only for looks. Nice-looking older women but not obvious targets. About seven percent of Burlington is Latino, so we're talking to a prominent community here. We've talked to family, friends... Nothing helpful so far."

Filman shepherded some crumbs onto his cupcake wrapper. "What's this about anaesthesia?"

"Yeah. That's peculiar. The coroner told us early on that these women were incapacitated with a stun gun and then asphyxiated. The micro bruising forensics were able to bring up suggests the killer used a medical breathing mask—the kind of thing an anaesthetist would use—to smother the women."

"I don't get it. Aren't those mask things vented in some way?"

"Yeah, of course. He must be sealing the mask or stuffing it somehow. The corner was even able to tell us the probable make of the mask from its outline. It's a common medical and paramedical brand: Osguard."

"Why doesn't he just use his hand?" Joshi shrugged. "So, this guy has gotten hold of medical quality equipment."

Joshi's chair creaked, telegraphing his discomfort. "We thought he might be using an Emergency Services truck, but that hasn't got us anywhere yet."

"What about a commercial patient transfer company? They've got trucks."

"Yeah, we checked that, too. Most of their staff are young women. I must be getting old; they look like teenagers to me."

"So…you're in a holding pattern," Filman said.

Joshi looked hurt. "Well, we've located the victims' cars in each case, but there's no significance to the drop-off spots that we can see. Different every time. Then there's the clothes. He probably dumps the clothes and jewellery in charity bins— again, a different one each time." Joshi poked his lower lip out, conceding that they had no promising leads.

Filman nodded. "A holding pattern then." There was a pause, but before Joshi could react defensively, Filman added, "Maybe you could take on a little thing for me?"

Joshi thought, *Aha! That's what this is about,* but all he said was, "Thing?"

Filman looked him in the eye. "A little silly season follow-up if your caseload isn't too heavy right now. There's a widow down on the beach strip. You know, the pedestrian pathway running from Lakeshore Road down towards Hamilton? She has one of those old cottages along the bike path. She's reported an intruder, a young girl on her basement stairs. She called it in," Filman wiggled his eyebrows, "twice."

"What do you mean, twice?"

"Called it in to 911 twice. I mean on two separate occasions a couple of days apart. Officers responded both times; no one there, nothing stolen. Basically, nothing touched."

Joshi sipped his coffee thoughtfully for a moment before, dripping sarcasm, he said, "Real heavy case you got there, Chief: a serial prankster! Public clamouring for an arrest, are they?"

Filman gave a snorting laugh and spread his palms. "Truth is, I don't know *what* the hell this is. The responding officers did a quick informal assessment to see if the homeowner was lucid, and she seems solid enough. Early seventies. Active in the community. Regular donor to the Performing Arts Centre. Likes musicals. Recently retired from teaching at a community college. She used to teach business, so not an obvious flake."

"You serious about Eilert and me following this up? We're Major Crimes. Are we being demoted to community outreach or something? Doesn't sound like our kind of thing. Why us?"

"That's just the point. It doesn't sound like anybody's kind of thing. I just thought we'd better cover our asses in case something's going on here. There have been plenty of serious break-ins of high-end properties down that way. It would be nice if we could prevent something like that before a really serious home invasion takes place and someone gets hurt."

Joshi shifted uncomfortably, wondering what Filman wasn't saying. "So, this intruder—a girl, you said—you think she's checking the place out for a home invasion?"

"Thought crossed my mind. It's not just any house, you see. The place is packed with valuables, big stuff. Not jewels. Mostly antiques. It could be a target."

"If the intruder's just a girl, why didn't the homeowner confront her?"

"Well, ah, the girl... She..." Filman picked up a folded place card advertising breakfast specials—*egg sandwich and coffee for $3.99, offer expires August 30th*—and began giving it way more scrutiny than it deserved. "...she disappears."

Joshi stared, allowing the place card a quick glance as though Filman had a comic script written there. "Okay, fine, so why aren't you talking to Eilert about this?"

Filman sniffed. "He's your partner, not your superior. Why do I have to approach him?"

"You don't, but he's up in our office at his laptop, probably looking professional and intrepid, waiting for the next forensic challenge to cross his blotter," Joshi looked down forlornly at his paper plate, "and I'm down here on break eating a banana walnut muffin."

He pulled off a piece of his muffin and suddenly frowned, his suspicions solidifying. "Wait a minute. Is this a spook? Is that what this is? I know what you're doing. You want Eilert on this because it's weird."

"*Unusual*. That's all. Maybe Eilert can think of a way to write it up for the records—show we've done due diligence. He has a way of making messy things…tidier. I don't know what we're dealing with: a break-in with nothing broken or stolen, an unimaginative prank, silent harassment? Don't spend a lot of time on it, mind you, but maybe you could talk to the woman. Look her over and see what you think."

Joshi rubbed his chin in agitation. "God. I can see it now. Eilert's going to be intrigued." He caught Filman's look of satisfaction. "Hey, that's *not* a good thing."

Filman laughed. "Say, I've been meaning to ask Eilert—that accent he has, very subtle and cultured and all, but I can't place it. German, isn't it?"

"That's what I thought, but it's sort of a hybrid he got from his German father, kind of a cross between Colonel Klink and Sean Connery."

"Sean Connery?"

"Yeah. His folks immigrated from Scotland."

Filman gathered up the plastic wrap from his cupcake and stood up from the table. "Huh," he said.

CHAPTER FIVE

Prem Joshi turned up the fan on the cruiser's air conditioning until it was audible over the road noise. "Last time we had a case down here on the lake, it was freezing. Now I'm dying from the heat."

"The floater in the shipping channel." Eilert Weiss, tall, narrow-chested, and sporting a longish moustache, nodded from the passenger seat, remembering the case that nudged his life off track: the impossible suicide of A.L. Rouhl that had turned into an equally implausible murder.

They rumbled over the lift bridge on Eastport Drive as they had back then, but this time Joshi kept turning left, choosing the streets that followed the shore of Lake Ontario.

The beach strip from Burlington to Hamilton had once been a scatter of cottages, vacation homes for the surrounding towns, and the roads along the narrow neck of land were just a shortcut across the end of Lake Ontario to Niagara and the United States.

Back when Burlington was a small market town on the long highway between Toronto and Hamilton, it had become a pleasant beach community with a magnificent sweep of sparkling lake vistas. There had been no high-tension wires swooping overhead then, no angle iron towers on concrete pads —only the promise of cooling summer breezes and Saturday afternoon picnics.

There had even been a carnival area for tourists once, where businessmen could bring their families and buy cotton candy and ice cream.

Back then, the big draw had been the Brant Inn which dominated the sharp angle between Burlington's waterfront park and the long beach that skirted Lake Ontario all the way down towards Hamilton. The Skyway Bridge that now soared above the pointy end of Lake Ontario hadn't been there; just a railway conduit carrying mostly freight but also the occasional steam-powered passenger train, an early precursor of urban transit.

Now at that corner was a wedge-shaped glass and steel pavilion with a flying roof that you could rent for weddings and conferences. "Googie architecture" the textbooks called the style, after the wife of a San Francisco restaurateur. Back then, Googie's San Francisco Eatery had caught the eye of an architectural critic, and the name stuck.

Besides the new pavilion, an expensive restaurant with tall windows overlooking Burlington Bay reflected the shimmering distance.

The GPS chirped and Joshi pulled into a narrow parking lot, one of several that served the pedestrian walkway in front of them. He parked beside a Jeep Cherokee. They both sat quietly for a few seconds, in no hurry to step out into the heat.

"Where's the house?" Weiss said, squinting up the bank at the trees and bushes.

"Should be easy to spot. I've got a picture." Joshi unfolded a photocopied image, flattening it atop the dash.

Weiss examined the grey image, picking off a piece of pocket lint. The photocopy showed a sprawling house inspired by mid-century Muskoka Lake cottages. It looked like it had been assembled by at least three different contractors who weren't on speaking terms. "Odd looking place."

"It's pretty old. A lot of these places started as summer cottages on the lake and grew by accretion; adding a room here and there, then a period of gentrification when the big money brought in architects to pull it all together. There was a railway line up there where the bike and pedestrian path is now. Fastest route between Toronto and the States once upon a time."

They got out and climbed the wooden steps to the walkway. On the lake side of the path, they could look down on the mismatched scatter of houses which suggested wealth and eccentricity in equal measure.

One of the houses was completely new, a windowed pavilion with a Cape Cod roof and the great shaft of a cultured stone chimney, but its neighbour still had the growth rings of its many expansions and extensions. Unlike the modern home with its gravel path and hardscaping, the older place had a garden with flowers at the back and a vegetable patch along one side. A flagstone path, as if drawn by Arthur Rackham and designed for Hobbits and humans, led down from the walkway to the house.

On the elevated footpath, they weaved around skateboarders and joggers until they reached the steps. From there, they stepped down to the gated fence behind the house.

Weiss raised an eyebrow at the wrought iron gate with its rusted quatrefoil ornamentation. "This gate didn't start its life on this continent, or in this century." He tried the iron latch, and the gate swung aside with an operatic groan.

Joshi unfolded his print again. "This is it, though."

"Have we established that the woman isn't delusional?"

"She's seventy-one and educated. Lost her husband six years ago, but she retired and continued to work part-time at Sheridan College until last year. What with her teacher's pension and the savings from her husband's antique business, she's fairly well off. She's lived here for decades. The incident report mentioned that the house suggests eccentricity, whatever that means, but Filman said the woman herself appears lucid."

"Okay. She's expecting us, right?"

Within seconds of their knock, Lizzie Collier came to the door in a sleeveless blouse and brown work slacks. She had a paisley sweatband around her forehead. She seemed relaxed and pleased to see them.

When Weiss did the introduction, she said, "I'm a little surprised the police haven't given up on me. Come in and I'll make coffee. Oh, and please call me Lizzie."

Weiss smiled his thanks and followed her into a high hallway. Lizzie Collier seemed well grounded somehow. She moved with an economical grace and her clothes suggested affluence with a complete lack of pretension.

"There have been a number of break-ins along the beach strip," Weiss said. "Good pickings for a thief, these lakefront places."

Lizzie stopped and turned to face them. "Is that what you're thinking? Burglary?" She shook her head. "She's not a thief. I can tell you that." She paused, still looking Weiss in the eye. "She's been back, you know."

"Yes, I understand that. Twice you say. That makes it unusual."

"No, no. I mean a third time."

Weiss had been checking out an armchair, ready to sit, but straightened up so quickly that Joshi stumbled against his back. "What, a third break-in? You didn't report it."

"Do you blame me? I knew what would happen. Another couple of well-meaning officers more interested in my sanity than the girl on the stairs."

"Yes, well, uh… What happened this time?"

Lizzie spread her hands. "Exactly the same." She gestured to the corner of the room where delicate wrought iron bannisters supported a teak railing. Behind it was a deep stairwell. "The girl stood right there, two steps down, just high enough so that she could see over the railing, and she started talking to me."

"Talked to you? What did she say?"

Joshi, having read the report, answered for her. "Nothing, right? No sound?"

"Exactly; just those lovely lips moving and that earnest, worried expression."

"Clothes, shoes?"

Lizzie narrowed her eyes, visualizing. "She was wearing the very same clothes, I think. A simple flared skirt and a neat white blouse. I didn't notice her shoes before, but I got close enough to look down the stairs this time and she had black and white tennis shoes on, a bit like the ones I used to wear to high school when I was a kid."

Weiss gave up on the armchair and walked closer to the stairs. "Show me exactly where you were standing."

"Sure. She was there on the stairs, and I got right up to… here." Lizzie now had one hand on the railing. "I'm getting brave, huh?"

"So, you were just a few feet apart, six maybe. Did you smell anything? A fragrance, perspiration?"

"Smell?" The question seemed to surprise Lizzie. "I…uh, no. I don't think so."

"It's been hot. Did she look like she'd been running? Was she tanned?"

"No. She… Well, I guess you'd say she looked stressed. She wasn't pale or anything, just worried looking. Nice skin. She's quite an attractive girl. About nineteen, I'd say."

"And she seemed to be saying what? Same as before? Mouthing it, I mean."

"Everything the same—every time she's shown up—over the course of, what has it been? Over a week now. And I have no idea what the girl wants."

Weiss looked carefully at the stairwell; at the way it went right down in a single flight to the basement level. The steps were solid in refinished wood, and the downstairs landing was old linoleum. He glanced up at the room lighting. "What time of day was this?"

"The visits have all been in daylight. Full sun from the windows over there." She indicated the windows fronting onto the lake, tastefully draped in sheers. "One right before lunch, and the last two in the afternoon. It was around two, last time."

Weiss looked around the room, baffled. "And this girl, she just disappears? Down your stairs." He looked at her, studying her guileless eyes and small mouth. "Lizzie, you strike me as a clever woman. You must see what this sounds like."

"Of course I do. I thought of that. It's no wonder you don't believe me, I suppose. I like a good ghost story, but this girl is no ghost. She was as solid as you and me. She even set off the motion sensor light on the lower landing. A ghost wouldn't do that."

"But you heard nothing at all? Not even her steps on the wooden stairs?"

"Oh. I hadn't thought of that. I should have heard her going down, shouldn't I? But it was almost like television with the sound turned off. Nothing."

"So, she definitely went down to the basement. The police report says that they executed a search, but have you been down there since this started happening?"

"Sort of. This last time I took the steps and stood in the basement, and I kind of called out to her. You know, I told her it was okay, that maybe I could help her. That sort of thing. But there was nothing down there. No one."

Weiss looked at Joshi without expression and shrugged. "Kids' prank?"

Joshi looked sceptical. "The girl is college age and kids that age do crazy…uh…stuff, but how is she getting in, and where is she going?"

Lizzie folded her thin, tanned arms above her narrow waist. "Yes, the police were interested in that. They checked all my doors and windows, and I assured them I always lock up, even during the day."

Weiss looked at her hand. Lizzie was wearing a wedding band and an engagement ring on her finger. She was a widow living alone. It made sense that she was careful about locking her doors.

He glanced up at Joshi. "That's the thing about magic tricks, Prem. It's all misdirection and illusion. We're going to have a look downstairs, Lizzie. That okay?"

"Oh, please do. The officers have been pretty thorough, but maybe you can see how the 'trick' is done."

Weiss led the way, Joshi smiling weakly at Lizzie before following.

———

The basement level had a fairly low ceiling, but it was a large L-shaped room with a pegboard wall on the short side, covered in tools and gadgets: ice tongs, a washboard… An old upright piano dominated the corner of the floor space. There was a dartboard on the long wall and a billiards scoreboard with sliding brass pointers, old enamel beer signs, and a scatter of folding chairs leaned against it. There was no billiard table.

Cutting off the corner of the L was a standing bar, complete with a brass rail that looked as though it had been lifted from a local tavern. There were liquor bottles on the bar—some full, some empty—displayed to one side, chosen for their nostalgic value with their labels still mint.

Behind the bar, filling the rest of the space and constituting the small foot of the L, was a haphazard wall of crates and boxes, piled almost to the ceiling. Weiss looked at it and then at Joshi.

"The girl has got to be coming from in there. How thorough were the uniforms in searching the boxes, I wonder?"

With Joshi's help, Weiss tried shifting the nearest crate, a softwood frame held together with wire and staples. "These are what they used to call produce crates," Weiss said. "Burlington was once a centre for market gardening—before the urban sprawl happened. I guess these were as common as cardboard boxes back then. They're pretty old."

Weiss laid his face against the right-side wall of the room, his short, greying beard flattened against the panelling. It was gloomy, but he could see most of the mid-century panelling right back to the rear wall. Lizzie's husband had left a slight gap there to prevent mould, and in the narrow space, Weiss could see the slight warping of the old pressed board wall panels. He did the same thing on the left wall.

Lizzie tilted her head to watch. "My husband was a collector, a dealer in nostalgic pieces. These crates were easily available and perfect for our stuff. The crates are full of…merchandise, I suppose he would have called it. We had a shopfront on Locust back then. When Clint got sick, we closed the store and the inventory we hadn't sold wound up back here at the house. We didn't know what else to do with it."

"Makes sense." Weiss took hold of a box the size of a small refrigerator. "Can we move this?"

"It has a Rock-ola jukebox inside if I remember. It still works. Clint said he could get three thousand for it easy."

Joshi took off his jacket and shouldered the crate, which was topped by slightly smaller cardboard boxes. The column slid a couple of inches along the grey lino floor. Weiss pulled at the stack beside it. It was heavy, but the crates were smooth and the floor slick, so it was doable.

"Let's spread them enough so that we can get to the back wall. I want to see what's there."

Joshi frowned. "Isn't this where we call in a bunch of young uniforms to do our bidding?"

"In a perfect world. Just push."

With a lot of hip and shoulder work, they managed to worm a space through the boxes. Weiss was thinner, so he was able to edge his way deep into the packed corner of the room, but there was only so much space, and the access was uncomfortably narrow.

"God, this corner of the room is jammed about eight stacks deep," Weiss muttered. "It goes right to the back wall, and every one of these piles is at least six feet high." He reached up and gave the panelling of the rear wall a slap. "But that's the back wall."

Weiss wiggled around, trying to get his bearings. He kept one hand flat on the panelling. "So, this wall would be on the lakeside, right?"

"What, the front of the house? Really?" Joshi looked around as if it would help orient him in the cluttered space. The only windows were in the open area of the basement, and they were small and high on the long wall.

"I think so. This back wall is like the others, made up of old-fashioned sheet panelling. Fifties vintage probably. You got a flashlight?"

"Jesus, Eilert, you're so analogue."

Joshi took out his phone and, reaching as far as he could, aimed the light on the sliver of wall Weiss had exposed. The panelling shone in fake wood grain and knotholes.

"Yeah, same sort of printed pressed board, buckled a bit with age and dampness. I'll bet nobody's seen this wall in a decade. Maybe more."

Weiss tried to wiggle open enough of a space so that he

could get a look at the entire back wall. Once again, he pressed his cheek to the surface. The back wall felt cold against his face.

Joshi stretched the phone as high as he could, but he couldn't get close because of his stocky chest. "Looking for a door, right?"

"The girl had to get in somehow. She's thin, lightly built. Maybe she could have squeezed her way in back here."

Joshi tried dragging more piles aside, but the stacks were crammed against one another, and the best he could do was wedge himself a few feet closer to Weiss. "So? See anything?"

"I think so. An old door frame."

There was a bit more shuffling, but Joshi couldn't see anything but Weiss's shoulder. "Aha! Yeah. It's an old doorway, all right. I can just touch it, but—"

Weiss breathed out his disappointment. "It feels like it's been bricked in with mason blocks." He grunted in exasperation. "Nobody got in through there."

"Any windows?"

"Nah. I thought maybe high basement windows, but nothing."

"That's unusual, right? A door facing the lake but no windows?"

"We're definitely below ground here. I want to go up and see this from outside. That door doesn't make sense in a basement room. Maybe it used to be a cold cellar. People used to use them for storing food."

Joshi backed up and waited for Weiss to wiggle out after him into the bar area. They dusted the shoulders of their short-sleeved shirts and turned towards the staircase. Lizzie was standing there wide-eyed.

"You have a lot of stuff in there," Weiss said. "Old inventory, you say?"

"I thought we might be able to open another location when Clint got well again. But he never did. There's stuff in there that's quite valuable to collectors, but you have to have a show space and I've never felt up to doing a liquidation. One of these days, I'll just pay someone to drag it all out and auction it all off. I won't get as much money, but I'm past caring. I just want it gone. I run a dehumidifier down here, but I'm sure it's not sanitary to have so much fabric and wood stored for this long. Mould, you know."

"I'm sure a lot of it is valuable." Weiss bent to admire the old piano dominating the open part of the room. "This is a beautiful piece," he said.

Lizzie's look of worry softened. "There's quite a story to that. In the old days, everybody used to gather around that piano and sing. It's a player piano, a pianola, but you could flip a switch and use it manually, too. There are some famous signatures right there on the paper roll. Jayne Mansfield, Jimmy Durante, Louis Prima, and others."

Weiss squinted at the wide roll of perforated paper. There were faint ball-point pen scribbles around the edges, but he couldn't read them in the angled light. "Really? How'd that happen?"

"Long story, but they were all down here at one time or another."

"Jayne Mansfield here? In *this* room?"

"Sure. With her little dog and members of her band. Back in the fifties that would have been. Members of her band were Black, you see, and they couldn't stay at the nearby hotels, so they stayed with local Black families and socialized with the staff of the Brant Inn where they were playing, and they'd come here to relax. You know, have a drink at the bar and gather around the piano to sing. Jayne was a classically trained pianist, you know."

"But why here?"

"The original owner of this house was one of the social directors of the Brant Inn. Benjamin something, I think his name was. He was the person who booked some of those famous acts—bands, singers, comedians… And he helped everyone find places to stay, including the Black performers."

"I'd like to hear more about that," Weiss said, "but right now, I need to know about that door back there." He pointed at the wall of crates and boxes.

"Door? Oh, the old doorway, you mean? It's not a real door anymore."

"Can you show me where it would be from the outside?"

"You mean where it used to come out? Sure. It'd be out front, but I may have a little trouble finding it."

———

They went up to the main room and then out a side door to the pathway that skirted the house and the vegetable plots. This led them out onto a flagstone patio that was getting direct sun. Beyond a fringe of tall grasses and a stretch of sand, Lake Ontario shimmered under a heat haze. High-tension wires ran along the beach off into the distance.

"It would have been there." Lizzie pointed at a bed of flowers against the house. "I think there were walls here and here, and the steps went down between them, you see? You can still make out the top of the walls."

"I get it. The walls are what they call earth dams, holding back the soil, but the old stairway has all been filled in."

"I think there was a problem with flooding, but it was a long time ago. I remember we were a bit worried about it when we moved in, but there was never a problem. The door had already been bricked over by then and tarred on the outside."

Joshi looked at Weiss with one heavily lidded eye. "Not to belabour the point, Houdini, but the girl didn't sneak in here."

Weiss bowed. "Thank you, Prem. Useful conclusion. And the police checked all the other doors and windows."

Lizzie blinked. "Oh, my! This is perfect for a detective story, isn't it?"

"How do you mean?"

"Well, it's a classic closed-room mystery, isn't it? How could the villain possibly have gotten in?"

Weiss grinned. "You sound like Carly." He assumed Lizzie would have no idea about whom he was talking. "That's a friend of mine who likes literary allusions."

"Carly… Not Carly Rouhl, the editor? I read about her helping the police around here."

"You know her?"

"Oh, not well, but we used to advertise in her magazine, you see. Nice glossy pictures. We had one spread that really looked classy: a palomino rocking horse on the most gorgeous shag carpet. Carly lives right up on Lakeshore, doesn't she?"

"The townhouses facing the park. Her father's old house. You're practically neighbours."

"She's quite the local celebrity, and I've read all her father's books."

"She's writing herself now."

Weiss was making small talk, moving slowly towards the back entrance. Joshi got there first and stood holding the door. The doors and windows were the only things about the house that looked new—the door, steel case, the lock formidable.

"Lizzie, there doesn't seem to be much we can do for you. I'll register the third, uh, incident. If anything else happens, maybe you could bypass 911 and just phone me."

Lizzie took Weiss's card and looked at it with her brow furrowed. "I see what you mean. Why take up more police time?"

"Lizzie, I'm sorry. I'm not dismissing you. I can see you're smart and honest. I just don't have enough to take further action. It's all about priorities."

"I get it. Not your fault." She moved inside to an old telephone stand near the door—a place to throw her keys or her sunglasses. Her new-looking iPhone was lying there, and she picked it up. "I want this to end, but…"

She tapped at her phone's screen for a moment while Joshi gave a discreet sigh and turned the knob, ready to leave.

"…I don't want you thinking I'm crazy like the others did. You at least seem curious."

"Lizzie, I…"

She turned her phone and held it up to Weiss. A video clip was running, dark but clear enough. A pretty young woman was standing on her basement stairs, her red lips moving. Almost immediately, the figure walked down out of the shot and the camera jiggled as the clip ended.

Weiss stared in disbelief. "That's her? Why didn't you show us this right away?"

"Like I said, I want all this to end. I wasn't even afraid the last time she appeared. That's why I had the presence of mind to use my phone. I fumbled a bit, so I only got a couple of seconds. At least now, when you write this up, you won't put me down as a nuisance call."

Joshi took the phone and replayed the clip, then handed it to Weiss, looking him in the eye, saying nothing.

———

When they were back outside in the heat, stepping up to the bike path, Joshi shook his head.

Weiss had been frowning at the ground, but he heard Joshi's slow sigh and looked up. "What?"

"The video… She's got you hooked now, doesn't she."

It wasn't a question.

CHAPTER SIX

Weiss parked the cruiser in the Village Square lot and walked with Joshi to the Queen's Head Pub a little way up Brant Street, an older establishment with fake half-timbering and an old English theme. They went through the glass door, Joshi sighing as the air conditioning refreshed him.

Weiss looked around. The pub was busy but subdued, as if the heat outside had exhausted everyone. The light was odd: little pools of window light and smaller blooms of table illumination that vignetted the heads and shoulders of young working people. Everyone seemed to have something to grin about, and abrupt scatters of laughter broke out here and there.

It took Weiss a minute to spot her. Carly Rouhl didn't quite fit the beery demographic. She was a little too private, like a celebrity in disguise; a little too much like a magazine fashion plate with her tailored clothes and self-consciously casual pose. Weiss had the odd thought that she had the air of waiting to be picked out from across the room by a special someone. Carly had the perfect booth for it, tucked against the far window, framed by the arch-like decals edging the window frames.

He remembered in the blink of an eye that he was the guest

she was expecting—Eilert Weiss, ageing authority figure and bringer of stories. He wondered if he and Joshi wore their sometimes sordid and brutal lives on their faces. But that was all right, because when he saw her, he smiled involuntarily, and that made up for Joshi's guarded vacancy.

She had her father's large mouth. On the old man, it had been a sad smile full of weary experience. On Carly, it was a joy, dominating her small face and, as her mind worked, showing a dozen shades of emotion in a moment.

Carly waved to them from beneath the street side window, conspicuously fashionable in her designer pantsuit and loop earrings. The light on her cream jacket was mottled with colour from the fake stained-glass appliqués high on the windowpane. In particular, the summer sun was playing a puddle of pale orange on her shoulder and dark brown hair while a green shaft caught her hands and the tabletop. She grinned and raised her glass.

Weiss nodded his pleasure, marvelling again at the way two crescent-shaped dimples framed the Rouhl mouth like parentheses when she smiled. Weiss sensed he was half in love with her, but it was a love firmly contained by realism.

"What are we doing in a pub?" he said. "You told me you don't like beer, and Prem and I are on duty."

"You said you wanted to meet, and I was shopping on Brant when you called. I get nice discounts from the downtown advertisers in the magazine, you know. The Queen's Head was close by." She smirked at some private thought. "Also, Evan has been taking me to some sports bars and pubs. I always order cider, but I kind of like the atmosphere in these places. Don't tell Evan he's winning me over. How's Toni?"

Weiss gestured vaguely with his hands, but Joshi answered for him. "Eilert's trying to be discreet about living with Toni, 'for her sake.' But everybody knows."

Antonia Beal, a Halton detective, had just separated from her husband of twenty years. Weiss had loved Toni for a dozen years. It was a love based on gratitude and admiration, and he still hadn't gotten used to being with her as much as he wanted —or at least as often as their sometimes-conflicting shifts would allow.

Weiss blinked. "Everybody knows?" To change the subject, he looked around, shaking his jacket away from his ribs. "Nice and cool in here." He nodded at his partner who looked marginally wary. "You know Prem."

"Hello, Detective Joshi." Carly clasped her hands primly like a third grader. "You might as well know—you intimidate me. I don't think you've forgiven me for all the trouble I got you into over my father's fake manuscript."

Weiss sat and Joshi wiggled in beside him, shooing him along the bench seat. "Guess you'd better call me Prem anyway. You and Eilert seem to be bosom buddies. But then that's my partner for you. Can't get in enough trouble by himself—has to enlist random members of the public."

"Carly's hardly random, Prem; she's a trained journalist with very useful skills."

"She's the media, Eilert." He flicked his eyes to her. "No offence."

Her fingertip drawing lines in the condensation on her glass, Carly sighed. "Actually, I'm leaving the running of the magazine to my friend Harriet these days. Technically, I'm no longer a journalist. Thanks to my father's estate, I'm free to write, and I've been trying my hand at fiction."

Joshi narrowed his eyes. "Fiction. I can see how that would help Eilert write up our more difficult cases. When the evidence doesn't add up, he gets…creative."

Weiss shook his head. "See, Carly? This is why I can afford to be so agreeable; Prem takes care of the cynicism and irony for both of us. Simplifies my life immeasurably."

Carly tried to suppress a grin, bowing her head.

"So, how is Evan?" Weiss knew Carly's boyfriend—first as a suspect in a murder case, then as a sometimes-useful consultant on document comparison and authentication. "Is his new TV show doing well?"

"He won't know for a while, but it seems to be finding an audience. You know: sexy personable hosts, B-level celebrities promoting their latest movies… I think he misses working with the courts on document analysis—he's a puzzle solver at heart—but he's enjoying all the attention. The poor man can't help being gorgeous, I suppose."

"Do you see him much?"

"The show wraps at noon on Friday, so he drives over from the Agincourt studios, and we get these long weekends together. Not a bad situation. Long term? I'm not so sure. We just agreed to take it slowly and see how things work out. You know, I think we're free to make our own lives, but it's not a straight path. You have to learn to grow around things. Like ivy on a wall."

Joshi, who didn't like similes, frowned, but Weiss seemed to get it. "And your writing's going well?"

"Yes. Strange, huh? It sounds like delusions of grandeur, but I think I'm becoming more like my dad every day. I've got an agent, and she's finding me a few markets. It's a start. Thank God I don't need the income. Dad's back catalogue is still bringing in money—even the autobiography we brought out last year."

"The one with all the photos. I remember. And the magazine's thriving?"

"Harriet is running the magazine well, as I knew she would." Carly looked at them both: Weiss was beginning to feel at ease, but Joshi was slouched back, waiting for something. Carly noticed and said, "What did you want to talk about?"

Weiss fingered the drinks menu. "I've got a good story for

you. Thought you might find it interesting. Do you remember Lizzie Collier? One of your advertisers?"

"Collier? Huh. I remember Clint Collier. Grizzly old goat, had a cute shop up on Locust filled with collectable trinkets. He ran a couple of expensive ads with us—full-page photo layouts. His rocking horse image was gorgeous. We had it sitting on a rug with a fancy child's top tipped up beside it. Do you know what a top is? Nowadays, everything's on a screen, but back then, kids were strictly hands-on."

"Sure," Weiss said. "I remember those. You pushed down on a handle and there was a screw thing that made it spin fast and wobble about. Anyway, that's the Lizzie I'm talking about. Clint passed away, and Lizzie closed the shop."

Carly waited for a burst of merriment at the next table to quieten before continuing. "I remember now. She was a college teacher, but she retired to their home on the beach strip—along with whatever was left of their inventory, I heard."

Joshi was looking about as though not paying attention, but he added, "Yeah, her basement is like a warehouse of treasures mostly packed away in boxes."

"Interesting. I remember they had some nice pieces. What's she going to do with all that stuff?"

Weiss took his opportunity. "Just the sort of question you could ask her, but you should start with her haunting."

Joshi grimaced, and Carly widened her eyes. "Haunting? Give me a break, Eilert. I'm not your friendly neighbourhood medium. You're making way too much out of my lucky guesses."

"Is that what you're calling them? Look, I'm just talking about a little side investigation Prem and I were assigned to that's annoyingly difficult to write up. There are no transparent ladies in shrouds floating six inches off the floor or anything— just a teenage girl with the trick of popping up in Lizzie's house and slipping away unnoticed."

"And she's solid, by the way," Joshi added. "We've got her on video."

Carly touched two fingers to her lower lip. It was her full, wide mouth that made people think of her famous father: the writer, A.L. Rouhl. On the old man, it could present as a piratical scowl but on Carly, it was somehow sensuous.

"Look, I have a great respect for creative instincts. It's what made my father's career. I'm glad my wild imaginings were able to help you on a couple of your cases, but I'm just a writer learning to trust my intuition. When you're in the business of making up fiction, you take your inspirations where you find them."

Weiss looked sceptical. "I have a theory about you, Carly. You have... Call it a quirk, where you know more than you know."

Joshi rolled his eyes, and Carly laughed.

Weiss persisted. "No, hear me out. I think you take in things —your journalistic training helps with that—and you file it all away up here." He tapped his tall forehead with its crown of greying bristles. "But then, you somehow put it all together in your subconscious and you find yourself knowing things without being able to explain how."

He looked out the window as a cyclist with a big, sculpted helmet whizzed by. "Someone told me you were my lightning rod. I'm not sure what he meant, but you've managed to clarify a couple of cases for me when they were going nowhere. I'm just a poor plodder trying to file away my caseload into the right databases: theft, murder, fraud. Now and then, that becomes impossible. The Lizzie Collier case is like that. Honestly, I have no idea what I'm dealing with here, and I wondered if you would at least talk to her. After all, she's practically your neighbour."

"And what? You think I might find a story in it?"

"A story? Sure. And at least you can *imagine* an ending to it, even if it is fiction. I don't think *I'm* going to be able to do that. Look, don't worry. This isn't connected with anything serious or dangerous. I wouldn't bring it to you if it were. Frankly, I don't know why they even asked Prem and me to look into it."

"You're stumped, huh? That alone intrigues me." Carly made a silent toast with her glass and said, "Fine. Give me her number and I'll call her. So, are you gentlemen going to have a drink with me? Some nice iced tea perhaps?"

For the first time, Joshi brightened.

CHAPTER SEVEN

Horst Schule, his blond, pigtailed wife, and his gangly six-year-old daughter were walking at Kerncliff Park.

They had reached the boardwalk, a wide wooden pathway that was raised above a patch of wetland. Near the centre of the path, they stopped and sat on a bench that occupied its own little niche, jutting out over bulrushes and tall grass. Katia, the little girl, was excited at the idea of spotting turtles in the few open bits of swamp water, and Andrea, her mother, was preoccupied with keeping her daughter from falling in. This gave Horst a chance to sag back against the wooden railing and enjoy the heat and the view.

To his left, there was the cliff that the park was named after, and it soared straight up to the railings of a cliff-edge walkway. Above that, he could make out Highway 5, Dundas Road, and the sloping hill up towards the Victorian village of Waterdown.

They'd come here before, even in the winter when the boardwalk could be slippery and the grasslands grey and sere. It was a perfect place to get away from the city—right on the edge of the city itself, at the top of the long gradual slope from Lake

Ontario. The cliff was a dramatic full stop before the suburbs took over and the cars droned by. If you didn't lift your gaze, you could pretend you were in a tidy little wilderness.

There were a few young trees that had established themselves at the bottom of the cliff, exploiting the very edge of the swamp. Horst wiped his neck with a tissue and revelled in this moment of family intimacy, Katia and Andrea babbling on about ducks and frogs and lily pads. He let his polarized sunglasses scan this part of his local landscape, a smile on his thin lips.

What caught his eye was the odd foliage of the spindly birch below the cliff. There was a clump that seemed to weigh down the silver branches so much that the tree itself seemed to lean slightly. Horst sat up and pulled off his sunglasses. It took a moment for his eyes to adjust to the glare from the cliff face, but when they did, he stared, and the smile left his face.

After a moment of stunned silence, he looked down at his wife who was leaning over Katia protectively. "Andrea! Take Katia. We're going back to the car. Now." He didn't shout; Horst was a self-possessed man, a manager who was in the business of keeping his head when everyone else was stressed. Andrea looked up, about to protest, so he added: "Please don't ask. Just... Let's go."

Andrea was pretty good at reading her husband, and the way she gathered up protesting Katia was almost as though she could tell her husband had just seen the naked body of a woman splayed across the branches of a birch tree.

———

There was no actual body in the room, no smell of decay or chemicals, but there was that large horizontal image on the wall screen. Weiss's office laptop was too small for this kind of consultation, so he was standing in the I.T. office with Joshi, looking up at a well-lit overhead shot of the latest murder victim—the woman found at Kerncliff Park, snagged on the lower branches of a tree that angled awkwardly from the cliffside.

"So, Alicia D'Alessandro." The voice from the speaker was clear but you could tell from the acoustics it was coming from a much larger room.

Weiss squinted at the image on the screen: a woman, forty-ish, with a dark complexion and black hair, cut to a fashionable wedge. He'd been there when the dusty, gravel-encrusted body had been hoisted up the face of the cliff. Then, she had been a bloody rag doll. Now, cleaned and serene, she was a sombre statue, her skin like Carrara marble. She had been attractive, he supposed—not strikingly beautiful, but she was trim, big-hipped and soft-looking, her plumb-coloured lips sagged into a thin grimace.

The image was live from the coroner's office at the Centre for Forensic Science in Toronto, and in an insert to the upper left of the screen was a balding man in a white coat and green apron. He was wearing rimless glasses and clear protective lenses were perched higher on his brow. It was a head and shoulders image, and the man's voice as he read from his report was cultured and English. Yorkshire, perhaps.

"We were thinking another ritual murder," Weiss said. "Do your findings bear that out?"

Doctor Reginald Binnie looked down out of his frame, the light catching his high forehead. "Don't know what else you'd call it. As I indicated, there's been no sexual penetration, but there are two marks on the body, there on the lower belly, which suggests some kind of vaginal fixation. They're burn marks. It's quite obvious that this is the same killer, but for due diligence, I did a micro-inspection of the burn marks, and from tiny irregularities in the impression, I can confirm that it was the same instrument that was used to brand the other women."

Weiss stared closely at the screen, recognizing the two small starburst shapes just above the woman's pubic hair. "He's branding his victims. Same location."

The figure in the upper left nodded. "Branding their dead bodies, yes. It's a kind of stylized eight-pointed star."

"Or a four-pointed cross," Weiss said. "It's ambiguous because the four chevron shapes meet at right angles like a cross."

"I see what you mean."

Binnie adjusted his glasses. "And then there's the missing breast, of course. That could just be an aspect of sexual sadism, I suppose, but given that the same exact disfiguration occurred on your two previous victims, I'm inclined to think it's either a message, or it has ritual significance. I'm thinking all the marks were post-mortem. Cause of death is asphyxiation, you see, so the disfigurements were probably done when she was dead and still. The star marks are aligned with precision and the breast was removed with careful circumcision. She wasn't struggling."

"Any idea why it's always the left breast?"

The coroner pursed his lips and made a wheezing sound. "Well, that's the one over the heart, so maybe that's significant. Your people have been calling this predator The Amazon Killer, or, by extension, The Archer. But the Amazons were supposed to remove their right breasts so they could pull a bowstring. That's the mythology, of course."

Weiss looked at Joshi with a "God, not again" frown.

"That's not my label. It just stuck for convenience around the investigation."

"The name got out to the media, though," Joshi said. He shifted and looked at the floor. "Wasn't me," he added for perhaps the fifth time.

"Anything else?" The coroner was jiggling a clipboard, signifying that he was done. He tried to put a pencil behind his ear, but there was too much plastic there already from the glasses, so he poked it instead into his breast pocket.

"So, there's nothing different this time?" Weiss asked.

Binnie sniffed. "Every body tells a different story, but from an investigative point of view… The other women were also Latina, in their forties, stripped of any jewellery. One had a rather gaudy nail polish, but that's hardly significant."

"Except that they were all well-manicured, well-groomed respectable women with children."

The coroner scratched his scalp, where the light caught it. "Well, that speaks to the killer's preferences, all right. He's not going for the usual sexual targets, hookers or glamour girls. Likes the mother figure maybe?"

"Okay…" Weiss began.

"One other thing. It looks like a smothering again with the same impression of a medical oxygen mask, but this is odd: There is makeup on Alicia's face, makeup that is not her own; transferred from the mask. The shade is different."

Weiss frowned at Joshi. "Maybe transfer from one of the other victims who was smothered with the same mask?"

"Yes, I thought of that," Binnie said. "But to have been transferred like that, the makeup would have had to be pretty heavy —almost theatrical, and I didn't notice anything like that on the other victims."

Joshi rubbed the back of his head. "You're implying the makeup came from another woman. A woman who wasn't one of the victims? How could—"

Joshi stopped himself. He was setting himself up for a rebuke from the coroner.

"Anyway," Binnie said, "there you are. The transfer follows the approximate shape of the breathing mask. Make of it what you will."

They thanked the coroner and watched morosely as the image disappeared and the screen defaulted to the Halton District Police logo.

Joshi stared at the screen. "So, there could be another victim we haven't found?"

"Someone who was wearing theatrical makeup? Seems far-fetched." Weiss shook his head. "It doesn't fit the killer's preferences either. He chooses mothers, doesn't rape them, but he draws attention to their breasts and pubis. Seems like a contradiction somehow."

"Maybe he's got a sexual dysfunction himself," Joshi said, "and he's taking it out on women."

Weiss flicked a light switch. The fluorescents above them popped on. "Or maybe it isn't about sexual gratification at all. They could be ritual killings of mother figures to achieve mystical aims—fertility, immortality? Foretelling the future?"

Joshi curled his lip in distaste. "Don't get ahead of yourself, Eilert. We've identified the four victims: We've got Abby, Maria, Carmen, and now Alicia. The local Latino community hereabouts is closely knit, so we may be able to trace the victims to a single Roman Catholic parish, right? We've already talked to the families of the victims, so we should talk to the priest, see what *he* can tell us. Maybe he can think of a male parishioner who's in spiritual torment or something."

"Well, that would be helpful. Might be interesting to know what spiritual dilemmas the priest has been targeting in his sermons, too."

"We need to revisit Alicia's husband; last time we were there, he was consumed with grief. Maybe he can think more clearly now. I'm looking for something that links the four women—a club, common friends, hobbies..."

Joshi loosened his tie. Even with the air conditioning, the

humidity made it feel close in the I.T. room as though the half-dozen computers were a scatter of waffle irons. "And then there's that symbol, the star. I want to research its significance."

"A star that's also a cross," Weiss said, holding open the door.

CHAPTER EIGHT

Jesus D'Alessandro went by the name Joe. His accent was slight, but he often paused in search of a word, covering it with "y'know" or "anyway." He was on leave from work while he tried to wrench his life back on some kind of track, finding help with his school-aged son and daughter—counselling, after-school care.

He was given to pacing slowly and lethargically, tugging apart the sheer drapes to look out into the quiet suburban street. Though the home was kept cool and dehumidified, he appeared to be perspiring. An expensive, tower-shaped fan sitting on the living room carpet somehow managed to silently rotate its airflow without visibly moving.

"Have the neighbours been a help?" Joshi asked.

Joe spoke with a slight, cultured accent. "They embarrass me with their generosity and, y'know, food and stuff. But we have family here in Canada now. My brother's family got a visa last February—so that's what I really need. Family is what the kids need."

He turned from the window, fumbling with a potted plant on a wrought iron stand. He got it steady on its base by gripping it more tightly than necessary so that his thumbs dug deeply into the soil. "Why is this man doing this to us?"

Weiss wondered who "us" was for Joe. His family, or his community? But he didn't ask. "Last time, I asked you about Alicia's routine. You said she worked from home."

"What I meant was that she drove a mini school bus, a twenty-footer that she parked here at home. She was home after the morning drop-off until the afternoon pickup. It left her free to come and go, and she… She *had* her own little car, that Kia in the driveway."

"She had lots of friends?"

Joe nodded. "Mostly through the church. She didn't have an office to go to. We would Zoom call to Nicaragua once a week."

"Did she belong to any clubs or groups?"

Alighting on a chair and immediately getting up again, Joe thought—stroking his long black hair back from his face. "She…" His voice broke a little. "She had a dance class every Tuesday and Thursday at nine A.M. She belonged to a ladies' church group. Something to do with, y'know, charity. That was every other week. The meetings weren't regular. Some guy would call or email with times."

"Some guy? You said it was a ladies' group."

"Huh? Oh, yeah. I think he was, y'know, like a contact person, a coordinator. He wasn't actually in the group she attended."

Weiss allowed himself a sympathetic sigh. "If you don't mind my asking, were you regular churchgoers?"

"Oh, yeah. Alicia got us all dressed up every Sunday."

"Would that have been St. Teresa's Church? The one downtown?"

"Mm, yeah."

Weiss looked at Joshi, who narrowed his eyes briefly. Then they were back to nodding sympathetically at this man who was on the very edge of despair.

Weiss and Joshi walked from their car around the front of the old church, their summer jackets hanging open, their white, short-sleeved shirts almost translucent. It was a large building but made of wood, painted white. St. Teresa's was several streets back from the lake, but some old variance had ensured that the land between the front door of the church and the lake be kept open, and there were a series of fenced greens spreading down to the lakefront park.

Joshi looked at the heat-stroked lake and rubbed his neck. "Odd that the church would be right down here on the lake. The property values are astronomical."

Weiss looked up at the neo-gothic doors. "It makes sense, though. The church is old, and back when it was built, Burlington was this small town crowded around the lakefront— from about the foot of Brant Street over to the hospital. In fact, the church isn't far from where the old Brant Inn would have been."

Joshi sniffed. "And Lizzie's."

Weiss turned to get his bearings: Carly's place a couple of blocks to his left; Lizzie's down the beach strip to his right. "Yeah," he said. "I suppose."

They walked through the big double doors and up a wide aisle between blocks of old, enclosed wooden pews. The air inside was cooler, imbued with shafts of colour projected from the windows. The vertical architecture and burnished wood suggested a community that favoured the past and old traditions. A couple of elderly women were sitting and talking in a front pew. They wore unadorned black dresses and modest hats on their carefully waved hair.

Weiss smiled and nodded. "Could you help us find Pastor Gusmán?"

"The monsignor's office is right through there," one of the women said in a pleasantly Meso-American voice.

The detectives knocked on an open door that was mostly

bevelled glass embedded with wire mesh. Pastor Gusmán got up from a large desk topped in red velvet. He was a red-cheeked man with dark brown eyes and wire-framed glasses. His hands, when he greeted them, were chubby, and his fingers soft and blunt.

Joshi sat in the available wooden armchair and Gusmán dragged another out of the corner of the cramped little office.

When they were settled and Joshi had done the introductions, Weiss held up his phone for Gusmán to see. "This is the star-shaped symbol I asked you about when I called."

Gusmán tilted his glasses and bent over the desk. "Oh, yes. I see."

"What do you think? Would it have a special meaning for a devout Catholic? To a member of your flock?"

Gusmán subsided back against a braided cushion. "Well, we have many symbols significant to the faith: the cross, the fish, the crossed keys… That one? Oh, dear. Give me a minute, will you?"

He rotated his chair so that he could pull a thin volume from his sole bookshelf. He seemed to know where to look. "Let's see. Knights Templar? Oh, of course. It's the star of Lazarus."

"Lazarus?"

"The man Christ brought back from the dead."

Gusmán laid the book open in front of him in a way that almost seemed devotional. He lined its Morocco binding up with the edge of his blotter and laid a hand delicately on the pages. "Yes, that's a pretty well-known episode in the Bible. Most people would be familiar with it, especially with our demographic. That's where the 'I am the resurrection and the life' passage comes from. It's central to all Christianity."

Weiss looked from the page to the screen of his phone as though seeing the marks for the first time—the four intersecting chevrons. "That's the line quoted in funerals and interments, isn't it? The resurrection?"

"Yes, exactly."

Pocketing his phone, Weiss asked, "What was that about your demographic?"

"Ah, Lazarus. Well, he's a particularly important figure for my flock because we have so many folks of Cuban ancestry, you see. Cubans celebrate San Lazaro Day in December. The seventeenth, I think. It's on our calendar if you want me to check. I recall seeing some of our ladies wearing the pendant of Lazaro, as they call it—your star."

Weiss nodded slowly. "So, in the story, Lazarus is taken from his tomb…"

"Yes, after he had lain there for four days."

"Then what? He's raised from the dead. What's the rest of the story?"

"The rest?" The monseigneur seemed not to understand. "You mean what happened to Lazarus after that?" It appeared to be a peculiar question, and it made Gusmán stroke his clean-shaven chin. "Oh, nothing important, really. He supposedly fled persecution in Judea and wound up on Cyprus. He was appointed a bishop by Barnabus and the Apostle Paul. As I recall, he lived thirty more years there and was buried…eh…for the last time. I'm afraid I don't remember any more of the story. You could look him up."

"It's pretty obvious though, isn't it?" Weiss said. "That particular star/cross symbol—it has to do with resurrection."

Joshi leaned forward. "Not resurrection. Cheating death. No offence, Monsignor, but the guy we're after doesn't want resurrection. He wants to stay alive. These are selfish acts of violence against women."

Gusmán recoiled. "Yes, you said this was about the recent… the recent…"

"Murders, targeting Latina women." Weiss pursed his lips, making his moustache bristle. "Selfish. Yes. But it seems to me you'd stand a better chance of staying alive if you didn't murder women on a regular basis."

Joshi persisted. "Achieving some kind of immortality then?" Weiss raised an eyebrow at him. "I looked up necromancy," Joshi said with a defensive sniff.

Pastor Gusmán's eyes darted back and forth; his small hands clasped tightly over his white shirt whose buttons were hidden by a vertical fold in the material.

Weiss let his eyes roam along the shelf of books behind Gusmán. "Do you talk about this theme in your sermons much? About returning to life, cheating death, immortality; those kinds of things?"

His hands unclasped, and Pastor Gusmán made a wide gesture revealing his soft palms and a wrinkled adhesive bandage at the base of his right thumb. "Well, the resurrection stories are most relevant around Christmas. And Easter, of course. Rolling away the stone from the tomb…"

"How about your parishioners? Any men asking you about death, worried about their health? Anything like that?"

"I preach to, and socialize with, around a thousand men at one time or another. Some are regulars, and some come and go. I'm sure they all have burdens, but no one in particular comes to mind."

"How large is this Cuban contingent you mentioned?"

"Cubans? Oh, dear. I couldn't tell you specifically. I just happen to know there are some because I've spoken to a number of families, and it came up. We have plenty of Mexicans and Central Americans, too, ethnically speaking."

"Could you give us the names of all your congregation? It might help if we knew the countries they're associated with."

"It's not that simple, is it? There are privacy issues with that. Not all of my people are on friendly terms with Citizenship and Immigration. And I wouldn't be the one to ask anyway. Were the victims of these attacks Cuban?"

Joshi answered. "No. Abby was of Mexican descent, Maria was Guatemalan. The last two, Carmen and Alicia, were second-generation Nicaraguans. But they all attended this church, and they were all recognizably Latina."

"Yes," Weiss added. "And they all left husbands and children behind."

Gusmán closed his eyes. "Dear, oh dear!" Then his eyes popped open, and he frowned. "I had a thought—perhaps you could talk to one of our laity associates. Our auxiliary. They take care of fundraising, social activities, and the like. Some of our ladies could answer your questions…if they were posed in a general way."

Gusmán pulled out a shallow drawer and set a small box on top of the book. He shuffled a few business cards inside. "Tell you what. I'll refer you to this man. He handles the phone tree for the auxiliary's executive. Besides the executive members, he would also have a list of donors. That's not every parishioner, but it's the kind of list you're after. He won't be able to just hand it over, naturally. What he'll do is put you in contact with some of the executives who might know more about the families."

Joshi sighed, and being closest, reached across the big desk. He accepted the business card. On it was the name Carlos Barnabé. It was a card from a company named Bathurst Properties, and it identified the man as a rental manager.

"Barnabé?"

"Yes. He's a widower. Nice man. Very generous with his time."

Weiss stayed still a moment, his tall frame slumped in the wooden armchair, then he started to get up. He said, "Thank you for your time, Pastor," and slid one of his cards across the desk blotter.

Joshi and Weiss left Gusmán absently stroking his Morocco-bound book and followed a short passage lit by a flickering fluorescent fixture. It took them out to the back parking lot. By unspoken consent, they each leaned across the roof of the cruiser, making eye contact. Weiss touched the white metal of the roof but snatched his fingers away when he felt the heat. He massaged his fingertips with his thumb for a second.

"How about this?" he said at last. "The killer wanted fertile women. What if this isn't about sex? What if it's about a mother's heart and womb?"

Joshi nodded slowly. "Yeah. Something like that. He favours mature women. I'm also thinking our guy is close—one of the churchgoers. I can feel it. If we could get a list of males and then sort by age…" He held up the business card Gusmán had given him. "This phone tree man might be able to help."

"It's not going to be that easy. I'll bet Gusmán is on the phone right now warning his guy not to put the flock under random scrutiny. Did you notice? Gusmán referred to the auxiliary as 'our ladies.' I think the pastor would rather that we stay away from the men of the congregation, and that's where our likely suspects are. Even if I manage to get the phone guy to talk about the male parishioners, I have to know what to ask him. Like, what age are we looking for?"

"I think the killer is ageing," Joshi said, "and it bothers him. He's got a huge ego, so big it makes others seem insignificant to him. He's devout but crazy, maybe even crazy enough that it would show to people who know him."

"He must be single," Weiss added. "He'd need someplace safe and secure where he can carry out his rituals."

Weiss went on thinking about that, letting his eyes wander out across Lakeshore Road towards the lake, which was blinding in the sun, but dark clouds were beginning to mass over Hamilton, drifting east. "You're right. We need to find someone living alone in a detached house. Preferably remote.

You can't smother women in an apartment building or condo. Someone might hear."

"But how is he getting the women to his place if it's so remote?" Joshi said. "What's the lure?"

"Maybe he's good-looking."

Joshi shook his head. "I have trouble seeing women with children falling for some gigolo's line. He's got something else they want."

"Okay. So, Abby and Alicia were working, Maria was a stay-at-home mom who went out twice a week to lead a dance fitness class—all comfortably middle class. What do you lure women like that with? What kind of offer, what kind of promise..."

Joshi was glowering at the moody sky, watching the way the storm cell was beginning to darken the lake when he heard Weiss popping the door locks with the remote. He reached down to the driver's side handle. "Something they're curious about or attracted to: glamour, fashion, celebrity...?"

Weiss took his time getting in. "What makes me wonder the most is that these women must trust him to some degree. Don't you think that seems odd? If we could profile the likely targets he's looking for, maybe we could put out some sort of warning to the women of the church."

"We'd be morally obligated to do that, but if the word gets around, we'd be forewarning the killer, too."

Weiss nodded and Joshi slipped his key into the ignition. With the engine running, Joshi hit the max cooling button and the air conditioning roared. "The thing is," he said, "the murders are getting closer together. He's getting confident, and he's got a system that works. We may not have much time before the next woman is taken."

CHAPTER NINE

From the church, Joshi took what he thought of as the faster route back to Number Three Precinct. Half by design and half autopilot, he went west to the ramp that would take him to the Queen Elizabeth Way east. It meant a multi-lane highway with overwrought drivers weaving in and out of traffic, but it was fast—usually. They were past the Fairview Drive exit before Joshi noticed the red lights coming on ahead of them.

"Something's up."

Weiss looked up from his phone. "An accident? Maybe we should check in with dispatch." He tapped the touch screen and spoke in a kind of monotone shorthand to a police dispatcher.

Joshi listened to the car's dashboard speakers, recognizing the voice of a woman he'd met in the precinct cafeteria. As she spoke, he scowled at his mirror. "So, a flatbed spill. No one hurt."

Weiss sighed. "But the mess could take a while to clear. Meanwhile..."

He craned his neck to look up at the sky, trying to make sense of the peculiar light. It was still hot and humid out, but there was some kind of inversion lying over them now like a tinted deadlight, giving the jam of trucks and SUVs a peculiar glow. It reminded him of the effects in photo editing software—sepia tones and hyped monochromatics.

Joshi turned up the fan on the air conditioning again and cursed quietly. Ahead was the featureless wall of a truck's roll-up door. To the left, a white Tesla looking like sculpted ivory. To the right, a panel van with a fancy graphic: N-Rite Plumbing Solutions. The letters were drawn to look like fitted pipe sections.

Traffic had slowed to a complete stop now, so Joshi had plenty of time to appreciate the clever ad. He shifted to park, sullen at the thought of all the unnecessary pollution, but he wasn't idealistic enough to cut the engine. Not in this heat. They'd die without the air conditioning.

Beside him, Weiss went on scrolling his phone. "We're going to get the run-around from these church people. I know that. The monseigneur will have reminded everyone in his auxiliary of their right to privacy—of *every* parishioner's right to privacy."

"He's just protecting his flock. But you're going to call around anyway?"

Weiss lay back against the headrest. "I'm thinking we may get a sense of the tallest trees."

"Meaning?"

"I'd like to have a sense of who's important in the hierarchy of laypeople—if there's anyone who stands out. We may not get the name of a potential suspect, but we may get referred to someone else who knows people."

"Yeah. Someone else who has been warned not to talk."

"It's a balancing act; they'll want to protect people's privacy, but they'll want to help catch the murderer. Besides, it's the referral itself that may be helpful. We could get a sense of the main influencers in the auxiliary. What I'm looking for is someone who knows a lot of people. We're not going to get anywhere just randomly interviewing parishioners."

"That's about as close to desperation as I've heard so far. Okay, so who's first?"

Turning in his seat, Weiss asked, "Have you got that card? The one the monseigneur gave you?"

Joshi dug it out of his pocket and took a fast look at it before handing it over. "This Barnabé person handles the phone list, and he's the only number we have right now. He's the gatekeeper, so to speak."

"Maybe I can at least get a few other numbers from him."

Weiss tapped away, and his phone purred over the car's speaker system. Joshi shifted into drive just long enough to inch forward a few futile feet.

"Mr. Barnabé?"

A man's voice answered, slightly accented in a Javier Bardem way but with a sophisticated enunciation that honoured every syllable. "Yes. How can I help you?"

"Detective Weiss, Halton Police. I got your name from the monseigneur at St. Teresa. He thought you could direct us to someone in the auxiliary who would know the congregation well. Someone who could help us in our investigations."

"People call me CJ. It's Carlos really." There was a reflective pause, then, "It's the killings, isn't it?"

"So, you know about the murdered women?"

"Sure. People in the church are frightened. They talk about The Archer on the news. It's that, right?"

"Yes. All I want from you are the names of some people I can talk to. You can do that for me, can't you? I just want to get a sense of your community; how cohesive it is, how supportive."

"Sure, why not." Barnabé gave the impression of someone wanting to help but nervous. "They're all good people. We all like to give a helping hand if someone is having a hard time. Grief, job loss, evictions—those sorts of things. But you've got to remember that we're the targets... The women are anyway. The killer is someone outside the church who hates us. I figure it's racial 'cause we're from Cuba and Central America mostly. The crazies are being encouraged by anti-immigration bigots south of the border."

"Is that what people are saying?"

"I've got the phone and email list, but I don't have a lot of social contact with the ladies. Let's see; Delana Brazos—she's the person to talk to, I guess. She's the president of the auxiliary and knows a lot of people in person. I mostly just keep the membership lists up to date. Phone numbers, addresses, emails. I've even got some social media on my lists. Can't go giving them out, of course. Privacy is a big thing these days. It's the web, you know. Identity theft... We're all wary."

"So, a number for Ms. Brazos?"

"Oh, uh. Just a sec." There was a rustle on the other end. It didn't sound like CJ had all the names on his phone. A laptop or tablet probably. To fill the dead air, he talked, half to himself. "Impressive woman, a real presence. Tall. Runs some kind of business all by herself, and you can tell." After a second, he read off a 905 number.

"Thanks," Weiss said. "I'm trying to get the big picture. Could you tell me how many names are on that list of yours?"

"Uh, I guess that's all right. Changes all the time, but right now we've got twelve members on the executive—mostly women because that's who tends to step up and help with social and support functions. You know, potlucks, guest speakers, food drives. Ms. Brazos can maybe tell you more. And there are 242 on the parish register. A lot more attend at one time or another, of course, but we don't have them all listed. Listing is voluntary."

"So, Ms. Brazos then—or will she expect Mrs. Brazos?"

"Oh, uh. I've never seen her husband if she even has one. Never mentioned one either, which I think is significant. The other women are always going on about their husbands and children."

"'Miss' then. There's no one else you think we should be talking to. No one that springs to mind?"

"Well, there's…" Barnabé was silent for a beat. "What do you mean?"

"It's just that sometimes our first instincts are useful."

"You're casting a wide net. You can't be making much progress."

"No, we're not. And women are dying." Weiss caught himself. His bitterness was showing, so he defaulted to habit. "If you think of anyone who might help us, please call Halton Police, District Three."

Weiss gave his name again, making sure Barnabé had time to write it down or tap it into his contacts list. Only then did he let him end the call. He looked across at Joshi, who was ready for him, narrowing his eyes.

"Did you get that?" Weiss said.

Joshi nodded. "The hesitation? 'Well'? He was going to give us a name."

Sighing at the looming, unmoving back of the truck ahead, Weiss turned again to his phone. He entered the number for Ms. Brazos and pecked out the new contact. He got a busy message and hung up, but Brazos called him back almost right away. Weiss wondered how much the auxiliary was talking back and forth with the news that the police were looking at their congregation.

"Delana Brazos speaking." Her voice was crisp like an actor, or maybe someone who had taken elocution lessons. There was a slight accent, attractive and exotic, but it had the guarded hauteur of a society matron.

Even before Weiss could explain what he wanted, Brazos went right on the defensive. Weiss barely had time to introduce himself. He hadn't even mentioned the murders, but she said, "Our people are the victims, Detective. I should have thought you'd be talking to the kind of people who wish us ill."

Weiss blinked out at the heat shimmering off the cruiser's hood as though Delana Brazos was standing outside against the truck with her arms crossed. He pictured someone dark-haired and dark-eyed, a stereotype from his subconscious. "I'm not casting suspicion on anyone, Ms. Brazos. I'm just faced with a problem: All the victims were affiliated with your church. Surely you can see that this pattern makes every one of your female congregation a potential target."

Delana breathed out slowly. "My God. It's true then. I mean, I knew, but I hadn't put it together that way." The steel back in her tone, Delana said, "Still, that doesn't mean the killer is one of us."

"Okay, so the question remains—how is a serial murderer getting inside your community to meet and lure women? If I could get a sense of how your community works... I do want to extend my sympathies; I imagine you had some contact with the victims. They fit the church's demographic, and they all lived relatively close to the parish."

"Just as I do." If it were possible to hear a shudder, it was there in the woman's voice. "As a matter of fact, I knew all the murdered women personally, and I'm devastated. Abby was a close friend."

"I'm very sorry about your loss. I'm guessing you would be the kind of friend who would help us catch Abby's killer. These women... They were all married; mothers with children. Is there any kind of connection among these women that occurs to you? Were they all on a particular committee perhaps? Volunteering in some way?"

"They weren't on the auxiliary. None of them were. I've seen them at social gatherings. A coffee hour comes to mind. Maria and Abby were both at our last one. Not Alicia, though."

"Did they have friends in common?"

"Maria and Abby had an extended social group, but I wouldn't be comfortable naming any of their male friends, even if I knew them. As soon as I name any male member of our congregation, he'll become a suspect by default." There was a shifting on the other end. "Didn't CJ tell you this?"

"He said he didn't know many of the congregation personally. He thought you would know more people."

Delana paused. "He said that? Huh. You couldn't find a more outgoing guy than CJ. He's a butterfly. Drops in on different groups and workshops to see what's going on, but he isn't actually in any of them. It's very helpful having someone on the executive with that overview when we have business meetings. CJ can give a quick thumbnail portrait of most any working group, having the lists and all."

"Is he after your job as president, do you think?"

She gave a humourless laugh. "CJ's not a leader. He has the charm, but he's..." She caught herself, realizing that she was doing just what the detective wanted—betraying the privacy of her friends. Back on the defensive, she continued. "The church is a refuge, Detective. Sometimes, we find ourselves protecting parishioners against the state and the bureaucracies. Some of our members have issues with immigration and health services. And racism, frankly."

"Maybe it's time you started thinking about mutual protection, too—within your membership."

A silence on the other end. Weiss thought he could hear someone say something in the background, but he couldn't be sure. Weiss got it. Brazos wasn't about to single out parishioners for his attention.

"There must be members of your auxiliary who had occasion to contact these ladies about event planning, fundraising." Weiss was casting about, trying to find a way around the wall of loyalty. "Perhaps you could give me the name of... Who would have organized the coffee hours, for example?"

"We take turns at that. Someone will order the urn, someone

else will bring coffee, someone else will be responsible for cookies…"

Joshi, gripping the wheel with both hands, snorted, and Weiss wasn't sure if it was because he was floundering, or Joshi's annoyance at the surrounding cage of traffic, but he tried another tack. "We've spoken to the families of the victims. Perhaps you could give us the name of someone who helps families in time of bereavement?"

Delana Brazos made some subverbal sounds of offended dignity. Nope, that wasn't going to work. "I fail to see why you are looking at our membership and the good people who help one another. Look for the prejudiced individuals who hate anybody they consider outsiders. Many of our people were born right here in Canada, and they still get identified as foreigners by stupid individuals who blame immigration for the ills of society. Look, I'll give this some thought. I will."

Weiss sensed he'd hit another wall. He let Delana Brazos end the conversation and slumped back in his seat.

Joshi had heard everything on speaker, and he sighed sympathetically. "She tarred and feathered you good. 'Course, she was right. The killer could be an outsider, someone who hates Latinas."

Weiss nodded. "We're not ruling that out, but if we go that wide, we have no leads at all. Murderers are often members of a family. This church is an extended family, and it's worth looking for connections there. Also, I'm struck by the fact that these women weren't young. And they were cherished members of the community—mothers and wives with no dark corners in their lives. Look at what we turned up talking to the families. Abby was a confident realtor working out of her home; Maria was a dance instructor leading a fitness group; Alicia drove a school bus, one run in the morning, one at two in the afternoon."

Joshi scowled at the plumbing van. "Common theme: confident, self-reliant, no fixed workplace." He dropped his hands from the wheel as though giving up on ever moving again. "Nothing. We got nothing. The women were homemakers in loving relationships. Abby was a work-from-home woman who hired a neighbour as a babysitter when she needed to be out of the house."

"Yes, out of the house. Abby only needed to be outside the home to meet clients now and then. Is that a connection? They all spent their days mostly at home? They all had husbands who worked in an office or factory and were away all day?"

Joshi nodded. "So…a door-to-door salesman maybe?"

"Who targets Latina mothers from a single church? He'd have to know them to connect them with the church. I'm still drawn to the idea that it was someone who knew them socially somehow, and if we're trying to link four separate families, that could mean the church itself. What else is there? What links four women at home most of the day?"

"Schools? Lawn services? Book clubs?"

The traffic crawled forward a few yards and a tow truck raced by on the shoulder, its lights flashing.

"I thought of schools," Weiss said. "But the women had children of different ages. Maria's son had started high school. They were all in the Halton Catholic school system, but none of the children shared a specific school."

"So, the church then." Joshi shifted into park to give his foot a rest.

Weiss looked at him. "Do you think I could get Barnabé to give me another name from his list? Suppose I asked to talk to the person responsible for… What…social events?"

He dialled the church's phone list coordinator again and waited while it rang. After a few seconds, he got a "please leave a message" recording.

"He's not answering. Knows it's me."

Joshi shook his head. "So much for the auxiliary. They've manned the barricades."

"Manned? Except they're mostly women," Weiss said.

"Yeah. Barnabé told us that, didn't he? What are you doing now?"

"I'm Googling CJ Barnabé, Burlington Ontario." The phone's screen was a bright spot in the noisy gloom of the car. "Hmm. Here he is in Canada 411. They've got his home address and postal code."

"That means he's working from a landline, doesn't it?"

"I think so. Point is, we could pay him a visit. He feels like a way inside the church's social structure. Besides, maybe he'll know men, and excuse my sexism but it's pretty obvious our killer's a male."

"You think you'll get any more out of him in person?"

"You heard him. He was about to point us at someone, and then he changed his mind. It's flimsy as hell, but..."

"Okay, so it might be worth pressing him. Where is he?"

Weiss tapped away some more on his phone, bringing up a map. "He's on New Street, near the Central Library."

"Okay. Too bad we'll never actually get a chance to visit him." Joshi looked about at the traffic idling on every side. "We're going to grow old and die here."

CHAPTER TEN

Carly Rouhl spent much of her day at a living room table in her Lakeshore Road home. There was a perfectly good office at the end of the corridor, but it was her father's old writing space, and when she was there, she couldn't get past the idea that she was writing in the huge shadow of A.L. Rouhl's fame.

The home she had inherited from her famous father was a comfortable row house that looked across the road to the lakeside park. There was the road itself—Lakeshore Road—and then the far sidewalk. Behind that, a low parapet and then the long stretch of parkland. In the summer, the park was often loud with children, music festivals, and the gaudy Ribfest. The one constant was the hazy horizon of Lake Ontario stretching from Hamilton Harbour to a distant metropolitan Toronto in the east.

Carly's row house was quiet during the week when Evan was at the Agincourt TV studios. It was from there he broadcast his noon talk show, and when Carly wasn't tapping away at her laptop, she would wander over to the window seat where Indy, her golden Labrador, liked to curl up. He'd lie in the sun, and she'd look out at the Skyway overpass and at the smaller lift bridge that served as an entrance to Hamilton Harbour.

This time, though, as she stood there, she took her phone and touched the number Eilert Weiss had given her. The phone purred and then Lizzie Collier answered.

"Do you remember me, Lizzie? Carly Rouhl. I used to edit *Escarpment Magazine.* You advertised with us."

"Oh, yes. I remember." Lizzie's voice rose, something between delight and surprise. "That's right! I handled all of our ad business back in those days. How nice to hear from you. My husband Clint had the personality of a used car salesman; he was happiest when he was haggling with some collector in person. He didn't mind me arranging sales and promotions. I was good at the books."

"I got your name from Detective Weiss, and I wondered if we could get together and talk."

It occurred to Carly that the story Lizzie had to tell might be more useful as a feature in the *Escarpment Magazine.* There were plenty of locals who would remember the store Lizzie and her husband had run. If she couldn't use the disappearing girl on the stairs as the basis for some of her own fiction, at least there was the "Where Are They Now?" story angle that would fill a column or two in the magazine. Maybe Harriet, the new manager, could dig up the original magazine ad with its fancy rocking horse. It would make a great graphic for the story.

———

And that's why Carly found herself introducing her friend Harriet to Lizzie at her home—the house on the beach strip. Lizzie greeted them wearing a flounced apron channelling some happy homemaker from an old sixties TV commercial.

An effervescent blond in her quietest moments, Carly's

friend Harriet was delighted by the little nostalgic touches around Lizzie's place. "Oh, my gosh! Look at this hat stand!"

The full flood of summer lake light flagged antique tin signs and mantel ornaments that seemed to be everywhere.

Carly couldn't help being impressed with this home, which seemed packed with character. She found herself wondering: Was it Lizzie's personality on display, or her husband Clint's? She tried to shut out the display of ad-covered place mats and lettered mugs, drawing Lizzie closer to the stairwell with each stage of the conversation.

At last, she said, "Eilert says you saw your girl here on these stairs…three times?"

"Well, that's what I told the detectives all right, but she's been here twice more since then."

Carly stared and Harriet picked up on her surprise, drawing near. Harriet pushed her glasses up her small nose. "What is it now then? Five times? That's incredible."

Lizzie laughed at Carly and Harriet's surprise and the way Harriet's eyes became huge behind her green-framed glasses. "One time, I was coming into the living room with a tray," Lizzie went on. "My evening cup of tea and a cookie—and I caught a glimpse of the girl making her way down the stairs like she always does when she's finished her babbling."

"Her soundless talking," Carly offered for Harriet's benefit.

"Yes. Exactly. So that time, I called out to her, but, as usual, she didn't seem to hear me. By the time I put the tray down and followed, there was no trace of her."

Harriet touched her cheek in a sort of old-fashioned gesture of amazement. In a way, Harriet seemed to belong in a room like this, with its aura of years long gone. Her fashion taste, while impeccable, was pure retro. The woman wore skirts, for God's sake.

"You're saying you followed this stranger down into your basement?"

"Oh, yes. I'm way past being scared witless. You should see this child—she's just a pretty little teenager. Not the least threatening. And it's not like she's a floating transparency or anything. She's as real as you and me. When I got down there, I could see that she wasn't in the main room. That meant she must have gone behind the little bar I have down there and into the storage area. So, I went there—I even tried moving some boxes around; trying to see where she had disappeared to, just like Detective Weiss did, but not a sound or glimpse of her anywhere. Mind you, most of those boxes are way too heavy for me to shift much."

"You said, 'once you were coming into the living room.' Sounds like you're not talking about the most recent appearance. What happened the very last time?"

Lizzie smiled with satisfaction. "Ah! I was ready for her at last. I've got it all here on my phone, only this time, I was careful to keep the phone handy and steady. You see?" She held up her phone proudly, taking it from a ribboned pocket on her apron. "This time I managed to catch her just as she was coming up the stairs."

"Detective Weiss mentioned a video...?"

"Ah, but this one is better—rock steady. You can see everything."

Carly's journalistic instincts kicked in. "What time of day was this?"

"It's right there on my phone, see?" Lizzie tapped the screen, reversing it for Carly to see. "3:18 in the afternoon—exactly. She doesn't always come at the same time, you understand, so I can't just sit around and wait for her. Anyway, I caught her out of the corner of my eye. She makes no sound, you see. So, I grabbed my phone and kept it on her the whole time until she ran downstairs again."

"Did you try speaking to her again this last time?"

"Absolutely. I feel sorry for the poor girl. I try to sound as patient and caring as I can, but she seems…inconsolable? Frustrated? I can't be sure."

"You said you can't hear her—do you think she can hear you? Does she respond to you in any way? Does she make eye contact?"

"Well, yes. She does. Looks me straight in the eye wherever I'm standing, but she has this defeated look, like she knows there's nothing I can do. It's like she's just unloading on me in despair. But, of course, I can't hear a word she says. Honestly, it's like a silent movie."

Harriet, who had been fascinated by the bric-a-brac of Lizzie's living space, rotated a glass orb in her hand—an insulator from an old power line she had picked up and forgotten. She looked up from it and blinked, mystified. "Does this girl seem bothered by your phone, knowing you're recording her? I mean, it sounds like you practically stuck it in her face."

Lizzie seemed surprised by the question and cocked her head to one side, thinking. "Now that's interesting. I never thought about it, but I really can't say. I think she glanced at it when I stuck it up between us, but there was no recognition there. It's almost like she doesn't know what my iPhone is."

Carly kept her eyes on the phone, watching the small image recorded in portrait mode before touching Lizzie's shoulder, focusing her. "So, you now have two separate video clips of the intruder. Am I right?"

"Yes. They're right here on my phone. The first one's not very good, I'm afraid."

Lizzie handed over her phone and Carly held it between her hands as Harriet looked around her shoulder.

The first time she ran the two videos without concentrating on details, Carly couldn't get past the idea that this was a stranger somehow crashing Lizzie's pleasant retreat on the shores of Lake Ontario, but after she got over the sight of an unknown teenager pleading silently from the stairwell, Carly began to notice subtleties.

The light was different in the two clips. In the first brief, shaky image, there was strong sunlight. Carly instinctively glanced over her shoulder to take in the nearest window with its view of the beach and a nearby hydro tower. She checked the time signature on the phone and said, "11:48. This earlier intrusion was in the morning. The backlighting from the sun sort of washes everything out."

Lizzie nodded. "You never know when the girl's going to pop up, so to speak."

Carly studied the second, longer video again, running it at normal speed. This one was steady and clear but gloomy, the stairwell a pool of shadow. "Was it overcast that day?"

"Yes. In fact, it was raining. The camera compensates well, though. If anything, the girl's clearer, don't you think? You can really see her lips moving."

"Was it raining hard?"

"Oh, well…steadily as I recall. There was thunder in the morning. It's the heat, you know. They're forecasting storms all week."

Harriet, who now handled much of the high-end clothing advertisers who kept the *Escarpment Magazine* in the black, poked her nose close, noticing the girl's white blouse. "Raining out," she said, "but she's not damp."

Carly looked at Harriet. "Right! So, she's coming from somewhere inside the house! She has to be. None of this makes sense unless she's somehow holed up in here. She's wearing the same clothes, wearing the same earrings, same belt as in the earlier video."

The decor forgotten, Harriet stared at the empty stairwell. "And this has been going on for two weeks now? It must be driving you crazy."

"It's unsettling, but I don't scare easily." Lizzie hooked a strand of her grey bangs over a chrome clasp. "I've been over every inch of the house—looked in every cupboard—but she always seems to come up those stairs from the basement."

Carly handed the phone back to Lizzie and put her hands on her hips. "Then the answer is down there. Can you show us?"

———

Showing her age, Lizzie took the stairs carefully with one hand on the wall. She led them into the panelled rec room, with its dart board and bar. Harriet was immediately entranced by the upright piano against the far wall. It could have been mistaken for an organ with its scrollwork, push pedals, and the levers that hung below the keyboard.

"Wow!" Harriet gushed. "How old is the piano?"

"It's a pianola, actually—a player piano, and it must be getting close to ninety years old. The paper roll with the music recording has a dozen scribbled signatures on it, including Jimmy Durante and Jayne Mansfield. There were quite a few celebrities down here in the old days: Patti Page, Johnny Mathis. Because we were so close to the old Brant Inn, you see. The Inn was a stopover for all the top acts that were touring through."

Carly left Harriet running her fingers over the paper roll with its vertical slots and walked to the bar area on her right. With her hands on the bar top and one foot up on an antique brass rail, she stood looking at the stacked wall of packing crates and boxes in behind.

"I mean, it sounds crazy, but there's only one explanation," Carly said. "The girl is somehow getting into one of those crates and hiding there."

Lizzie gave a half-hearted laugh. "You mean she's in there now like some cornered raccoon? But that's absurd. There're only five or six boxes big enough for her to fit in, and they're all packed full with our old inventory."

Carly moved in past the bar and ran her palm over one of the largest cardboard boxes. "What about this one?"

"I know exactly what's in there. It was a long time ago, but I packed it myself."

"What's in it?"

"It's our largest item: a Panoram."

"Panoram?"

"Yes. A real gem, worth maybe four thousand dollars in an auction."

Carly's blank look made Lizzie go on. "Most people don't remember, but Panorams were popular in the late thirties and early forties. They're like a big jukebox, but they play a loop of film for a nickel a go, complete with sound. Kind of like an early television. There's a regular jukebox in there, too, in another crate: a 1950s Rock-ola. It plays twenty 78 r.p.m.'s, and there's a music stand from the Stan Kenton Orchestra. You know, one of those things that the trumpet players set their music on? They were all matched and they had the band logo on them. There's a large wall mirror with some beer advertising in that one on the left and a big, folded table parasol from the Sky Club. That was the outdoor patio behind the old Brant Inn. And…"

Lizzie stopped, aware that she could go on cataloguing for an hour.

Carly glanced back at Lizzie. "Yes, you were saying your house is close to the site. The Inn used to be up on Lakeshore near where I live. I've heard about it."

"A lot of our collectables came from there. We scooped them up when the place closed in the sixties. It's amazing the treasures we were able to save from the demolition."

Harriet came over, looking pleased. "Hey, Car. This has the makings of a feature spread for sure."

Refusing to be distracted, Carly asked, "Are there any of the other large crates with enough room for a young girl to squeeze into? Maybe one with a lot of crushable fabric in it. Just enough space for her to sleep?"

"I don't see how that would be possible." Lizzie scoffed, unwilling to take the idea seriously but eying the pile of boxes and crates. "There's nothing in there that would be soft enough, and the wooden crates are all stapled shut. All of the cardboard boxes are taped with that clear plastic tape. The idea of someone crawling in there seems absurd."

"I know it does," Carly conceded. "How would she eat? But when you're faced with an absurd situation, you have to consider everything." She walked over to the old pianola, tracing the scrollwork above the keys with her finger. "Lizzie, have you ever thought…"

Lizzie stood behind her, waiting. "What's the matter, Carly? You look worried."

"Your house is lovely, and it's filled with interesting things."

"There's something about it that bothers you. I can tell."

"It's just that… Have you ever thought about just how much of the past there is around you?"

"You mean my collection."

"It is a collection, but it's not a collection of spoons or concert posters. It's the past itself. I'm talking about the decor upstairs…and the memories packed away in these crates."

Lizzie laughed. "What, you think I'm trapped in the fifties or something?"

"Well, you see what I mean. Can you be happy being…fixed to a time long gone?"

"Dragged down by it, you mean."

"I'm sorry, Lizzie, but I see you as an active, interesting person, someone who goes out and meets people. You told me you even watch my boyfriend Evan's dreadful interview show with all those self-absorbed celebrities. So, you're aware of the world out there.

But then, here you are in your vintage house with all its memories of a long-gone market town by the lake, and all these icons of post-war life—the dishes, the trays, the posters, the basement full of boxed-up Americana. How can you fully live in the present?"

Lizzie frowned. "They're just *things*, Carly. You take them too seriously. Everything we buy, everything we surround ourselves with—well, they're all a drag on us, I suppose. My heavens! What about *your* house? Everyone's seen pictures of your father's little office. If that isn't an anchor to the past, I don't know what is."

"You're absolutely right. And that's probably why I'm worried about you. I'm used to it, you see. I'm used to the past weighing me down. My father lived and wrote—not so much from direct experience as within his memory. I used to see him sitting there at his desk, staring at his wall of books and memorabilia, and he was in another time. Do you see what I mean? He was a chronic nostalgic, if that's even a word. He didn't much care about the present, and the present is where I've always tried to live."

"Oh, my gosh, that hurt you, didn't it? That he wasn't present for you."

"He wasn't a bad father; just distant. He drank pretty steadily, but he wasn't cruel or abusive—just kind of not quite there. I often wondered what he saw when he gazed off into space; his books were full of people and places, half-remembered, half-made up. I've always been fascinated, not just by the images he conjured up in his head but *by how* he did it. He was supposed to be a travel writer, but I said to him once that he was a time traveller. He just laughed, of course.

"I knew that, in his mind, he was weaving truth in with fiction. I suppose it's why I'm a writer, too. I was a good editor, you know, but what I'm doing now—writing fiction—there's a touch of the mystical about it, in my own head at least. I catch myself staring off the way he used to, and sometimes it scares me…like I'm going someplace he used to go."

Harriet turned to Lizzie. "Despite what she says, Carly's pretty grounded. I can tell you about her editing skills. She's got a good head for business, and she made that magazine thrive. I'm just keeping it going."

Carly smiled at the compliment. "But now here I am, becoming more like my father, staring off into my own dream-like space, imagining stories—things that I make up out of…you know…memories."

"But you're happy," Lizzie said. "Aren't you?"

"I should be. Thanks to my father, I've got financial security, and I've got a man who's goofy enough to love me. But," Carly's jaw dropped a bit, her lips parting, "I'm always afraid."

"Of what?"

"Well, of that room of my father's for a start. That place is like a mausoleum to me."

Lizzie struggled to understand. "Why don't you renovate or sell the house?"

Harriet had heard the argument before. "That's harder than you think. There's talk of designating Carly's house as a historic site, and there's a film company that wants to use his office as the centre point of a documentary about A.L. Rouhl. God knows I've visited enough sites of literary history to understand: Dickens's house, Dylan Thomas's cottage, Jane Austen's tomb at Winchester…"

Lizzie got it. "I think I know what's going on here. You're projecting—worrying about me. That's sweet. But whatever is going on here, *I'm* not afraid."

"But what if you *should* be? Not of the girl, but… I've felt it myself. I felt it the first moment I walked into your living room."

"What are you talking about?"

"It's like… It's like a…" Carly struggled with the thought. "Have you ever been under anaesthetic? You're awake, aware of your surroundings and then... There's a line from Coleridge: 'A drowsy numbness dulls my sense, as though of hemlock I had drunk.' Does this sound crazy? When I touch this old pianola of yours, I imagine I can feel other fingers on the keys, the pumping of feet on the pedals. I know it's just imagination, but sometimes I feel like I don't control it. You've heard of people letting their imaginations run away with them?"

Harriet touched Carly's arm. "Let's go upstairs."

But Carly went on brushing the keys. "And then the room begins to feel unreal. Tenuous?" At last, she looked up and tried to sound practical. "My point is, your house is lovely, but maybe just a little...dangerous. Maybe you should have a big auction and lift some of the weight off your soul."

———

Upstairs, with lemonade in a vintage soda shop glass, Carly felt embarrassed by her ramblings. Lizzie put on a floor lamp to dispel the gloom from the overcast, but it didn't help. She saw Carly staring at the lamp.

"Yes, you're right," Lizzie admitted. "It's mid-century modern—a George Nelson bubble lamp. I do sell some of this stuff, you know. I've had some success with Facebook Marketplace, but I'm really not comfortable with all that technology. Maybe there *is* something wrong with me; I'm a child of another time, and maybe I'm a little too caught up in my memories."

She shrugged an apology. "But these things... They make me happy. Clint and I were happy, too. We started collecting when we were relatively young. Even then, we had a sense of the old ways and the old icons slipping away, becoming oddities that people would buy as sort of a defence against change. Sometimes, I'll look at a mug or a poster that Clint saved from somebody's barn, and I can almost imagine him standing here with me."

Carly winced as though Lizzie had touched a nerve. "I've got to tell you, Lizzie. I'm not a believer in ghosts. Couple of years ago, after my father died, I had the irrational sense that he was still somehow manipulating my life, trying to protect me. But even then, there were no apparitions, no walking spectres."

Carly glanced at Harriet. A few months ago, Harriet had seen Carly lapse into a kind of waking dream and appear to talk to an imagined presence. She pulled her green eyeglasses forward and looked over the frames at Carly. "And what about your visions?"

Lizzie's eyebrows went up. "Visions?"

Carly shot an exasperated glance at the ceiling. "I've had a couple of…uncanny waking dreams where I imagined things that weren't there, but I know the difference between a daydream and an apparition. If you've read my father's stuff, you know he was something of an expert on ghost stories. We used to toss plot ideas around from time to time."

Harriet, who had read everything the old man had published, lit up with enthusiasm. "My favourite was the story about the lighthouse keeper in Maine—"

But Carly cut her off. "Dad had an idea that ghost stories were really about time. For him, it was all about time. He used to quote Einstein: Time is a persistent illusion."

Lizzie repeated, "Time?"

"I don't want to get into it, but he had some peculiar notions about time and the way it rules our lives. To hear him tell it, ghosts are nothing but people freed from the constraints of passing time. He would say that they see things differently than we do—past, present, future all muddled up together."

"Did you never wonder?" Lizzie asked.

Carly gave a bitter laugh. "Dad and I, we were writers— literary nerds who liked to play with plot devices. I always thought his take on ghost stories was lame. Notions of time aside, how do you write a good ghost story if your ghost can't *do* anything in the real world? All Dad's 'ghosts' had going for them was their lofty perspective, looking at the flow of time from the outside, so to speak." Carly frowned. "Hey! Why are we wasting our time talking about supernatural nonsense? We've got a flesh and blood young girl, and all we know is that she keeps coming up your stairs to this room. *And* we've got video."

CHAPTER ELEVEN

Carly could never quite understand what set Evan off. He would look at her while she was doing something mundane like loading the dishwasher and the next thing she knew, she was on the counter with Evan between her legs, pulling her head down into a kiss. He seemed to corner her at the most unlikely times —in the middle of a TV news show or after an afternoon cup of tea. She loved his attentions, but there were times, like this morning, when it could be embarrassing.

Around eleven, there was a knock on the door and Carly had to find a way of re-hooking her bra with her blouse still buttoned up. She squeezed past Evan, who was straightening his shirt, and made for the front door. Indy was way ahead of her, bouncing unhelpfully around the front hall.

Carly gave her blouse one quick shrug and opened the door.

Lizzie stood on Carly's front step framed by the light from the lake. She was immaculately dressed, as though this was a major social event for her, but anyone looking closely would notice the way Lizzie held fast to the fashions of her youth. The summer jacket over her round-necked blouse was a muted plaid design, and her slacks were wide at the ankle.

"I'm not too early, am I?" she asked, picking up on the way Carly was straightening her hair.

"No, you're right on time. Evan has the TV set up so that we can watch the videos together. Come and meet him."

Evan came out of the kitchen beaming as though nothing out of the ordinary had possibly happened in there. Perhaps, Carly thought, beaming a bit too much.

Lizzy's eyes widened. "Oh, my goodness. Carly told me. You're the Evan Favaro on the TV! The noon show!"

Carly was used to the way people, especially women, would gush over her boyfriend. Most women would be pleased with this, but Carly found it irritating. In fact, she was inclined to see the whole celebrity TV thing as a distraction, luring Evan away from his gifts as a researcher and expert on textual analysis.

She'd gotten past her impression that Evan was shallow—she'd seen the kind of resourcefulness he was capable of, but she couldn't quite forgive him for being so damned good-looking. Carly thought of herself as attractive; she had large dark eyes and interesting lips (a trigger for Evan's sudden attention, she suspected), but it was as if on-screen folk were on a whole different scale of beauty, starting from where mere mortals like herself left off. It was lucky she was a sensible woman capable of steeling herself against Evan's video-ready chin and bankable shoulders.

"Evan's not just decorative, fortunately. He does seem to like making small talk with tattooed recording stars and internet influencers, but I sometimes manage to remind him he's had a useful education. Evan has helped the police with everything from disputed documents to handwriting analysis. If he could just stop earning scads of money as a media personality, he still might make something of himself."

Evan made a near kiss of Carly's hand. "Carly thinks she's saving me from my ego. She doesn't appreciate how pathetically insecure I really am."

Carly ignored him. "Would you like coffee, Lizzie? We're set up in the living room."

Lizzie spent a moment fussing over Indy, who had taken to the new guest. Evan wasn't the only glamour boy in the house; Indy had a profile that would set dog show judges' hearts aflutter. Then Lizzie turned her attention to the fact she was in a historic house. "Do you think I could see the room where your father wrote all those famous books?"

"Ah! The room." Carly sighed but was happy to oblige. All her visitors made the same request, and Carly was proud of her father's genius.

They made their way down a short hallway to the end. "This is it. The great man's inner sanctum." Carly stopped and pulled a small strip of blue paper from the door frame. It had a tiny tassel attached to one end.

Lizzie peered at it. "What's that?"

"It's just a bookmark. I slipped it into the frame of the door this morning. I've had a little trouble with the door sticking and I wanted to see if the gap around the door was expanding and contracting. I should get the door rehung or shaved or something. I'm hopeless with carpentry, and Evan's worse."

After a tiny hesitation that few would notice, Carly took the doorknob in hand and turned it. The panelled door whispered aside, and Carly stepped back so Lizzie could go in first.

Lizzie's eyes went wide as she stepped inside onto a braided rug. And there it was—the desk of A.L. Rouhl: author, literary lion, and national treasure. There was a laptop on the desk, open but inert. Carly left it there, afraid to move it, as though it was the centrepiece of a museum diorama.

But as Lizzie gazed respectfully at A.L. Rouhl's blotting pad and the token bottle of Port that Carly left there, unopened, Carly leaned against the door frame, trying to put her father's suicide out of her mind. The doorway was just wood and house paint, but against her back, it felt like an isobar between the present and the past.

Suicide or murder? It had been a violent death—a self-inflicted gunshot wound—and it had occurred in this same room. Carly smiled at Lizzie's worshipful absorption, trying to resist the air of mystery that still pervaded the wall of books and cluttered mementos that were everywhere.

"You and I have something in common, Lizzie. We're surrounded by fragments of the past."

Lizzie laughed. "That was all Clint's doing—all those collectibles at my house. If it hadn't been for Clint, I'm sure I would have been a very dull accountant. Clint made my life rich —but messy. He was worth the mess, though."

Carly smiled sadly. "I sometimes worry that if you get too much of the past crammed around you, it goes critical like a nuclear reactor."

"And then what happens?"

Carly turned the blue bookmark in her hands sheepishly. "Well, in the case of a writer like me, my imagination can some-times get the better of me."

"You don't have to worry about me, dear. I'm afraid I don't have much of an imagination. I certainly couldn't have imagined anything like our girl on the stairway, despite what the police might think."

"I don't see how anyone could think you imagined her now. Let's go into the living room and take a good hard look at this cheeky kid on video and figure out what she's doing on your staircase."

Lizzie didn't quite pick up on Carly's enthusiasm, holding back for a few seconds with her hand on the desk. Indy trotted in and took up his accustomed spot on the rug. "That's what this girl is, isn't she? She's like a silent video; no sound, no smell... Just an image."

Carly waited a second and then waved a hand at Indy. "C'mon, big fella. Out of here. Go find Evan."

Lizzie smiled and followed. Carly swung the office door behind her. She took a quick glance behind her to see if Lizzie was watching, then slipped the bookmark back in the door frame, jamming it tight with a sharp tug.

On the big screen of Carly's smart TV, the girl looked alarmingly close. Lizzie's iPhone had given an impression of a frail, shadowy young woman with a heavy sadness about her. Blown up to something approaching life-size, she was a solid presence. You could see the slight puckering of her delicate brow, the almost imperceptible narrowing of her eyes signifying emotional pain. She was solid, all right. They could see the subtle modelling of her form in the ambient rain-soaked light from Lizzie's lake-facing windows.

Standing together in Carly's living room, Carly, Evan, and Lizzie watched the two videos, the second much better than the one before, as Lizzie's hand had grown steadier and her eye bolder. Lizzie was an unseen presence on the recordings, her off-screen voice at first tremulous, then reassuring, then demanding: "What do you want from me?"

None of Lizzie's recorded words did any good, of course. The girl went through the same motions, mouthed what seemed to be the same silent words, and stayed at about the same level on the stairs before chugging down the steps to the basement landing.

In her third video, Lizzie had obviously tried to follow the girl, rounding the bannister, and taking the steps a few feet behind the girl. The phone camera bounced as Lizzie started down, but from Lizzie's viewpoint, they could see the girl's summer blouse, so light and translucent a white that you could see the hint of her bra strap against lightly tanned skin. There was a brief confusion of light and dark, and then—

"Do you see that?" Lizzie exclaimed. "It almost felt like I'd succeeded in following her into the basement, but suddenly the girl was gone."

"You're saying she just disappeared?"

"Don't get me wrong. It was nothing dramatic; she didn't literally disappear or fade to a wisp or anything like that. It was just the way the shadows in the narrow staircase worked; she got lost in shadow for the merest second, then the motion sensor turned on the basement light and when I blinked at the harsh light, she just wasn't there anymore."

"Do you think she had time to run to the packing crates?"

"Well…no. I wouldn't have thought so. I went right in after her."

The video ended, and the big TV screen went dark. Carly stared at her feet; her thumbs hooked in her designer jeans. She couldn't allow herself to agree with Lizzie's assessment that the girl had somehow vanished.

"She must have bolted across the room and into the crates. It's possible."

Lizzie was picking up the frustration in the room. "I think the motion sensor light scared me for a second," she apologized.

"Okay," Evan made a calming gesture, "we need more information, and the only way we're going to get it is by looking more closely."

He ran the best clip two more times. Having transferred the video to his tablet, Evan was playing with the feed by stroking his fingers on the iPad, getting close-ups of everything from the girl's hand on the railing (no ring) to her ears (simple pearl studs). Carly watched half-heartedly.

———

Lizzie got tired first, and she sagged into an armchair. The afternoon passed and, what with lunch and talk, it was getting on towards evening, so the three of them had tea around the window seat while tourists in shorts and tees wandered by outside on Lakeshore Road. Evan was becoming something of a professional schmoozer—one of the things Carly didn't like.

He was charming and good-looking in an effortless way that sometimes amused, sometimes annoyed Carly, as though her affection for him was somehow a sign of her shallowness. Lizzie, of course, gushed over Evan's stories of celebrity guests and life in the public eye. "Jason Priestly is quite a nice person..."

Evan offered to take Lizzie home in his sporty hybrid Acura, but it was such a pleasant walk through the park, around past the Jo Brant Hospital and down on the lakefront trail, that Lizzie insisted on going by herself in the relative cool of the onshore breeze.

She picked up her dry umbrella in the front hall. "It's supposed to rain later. Meanwhile, the umbrella makes a fine parasol."

Lizzie gave Carly a quick cheek press and made her way spryly down the front steps. Carly watched from the doorway for a minute until she felt Evan's hand slip inside her waistband. Evan's hands were like the rest of him: smooth, elegant, and manicured. He could have done hand cream commercials. At that moment though, his right hand felt huge. That prim and dignified part of Carly's mind that she seldom silenced was making a note to ask him if he had ever played basketball.

———

"Impressive woman," Evan said. Rebuffed by Carly for now, he moved to the living room window to watch Lizzie cross the road to the park.

Carly stood behind him. "In her own way, Lizzie's very acute. I get the impression she was the brains behind the collectibles business; made it profitable at least. Her husband was what we'd now call a picker. From what she tells me, for Clint, it was all about the hunt. He spent days on the road here and in the States, snapping up bargains."

Evan turned from the window, growing thoughtful again. "Don't you think the most amazing thing in all this is that Lizzie never heard a sound in all her time with the girl?"

Carly nodded slowly, catching the significance. "She never heard a sound, never sniffed the girl's perfume, never got to touch her."

"So, all we've got is the visual."

"That's all we have—a good solid look at the girl. Just the two phone videos."

"That last one is pretty good. All you could ask for, really." Evan went back to the living room and turned on the TV again. He opened the file that he had transferred to his iPad and there was the girl again, freeze-framed in 4K. "Good, clear image— look, you can see her hair clip."

Carly was reluctant to study the screen again. She felt weary, having gotten nowhere with the repeated viewings. By contrast, Evan looked almost fierce, staring down the image like a prosecutor.

"Oh, yeah," Carly conceded, raising an eyebrow to take in the hair clip. "Hard plastic. I had one just like that once."

Evan looked at her. "How long ago?"

"What?" Carly sat on a dining room chair, wondering at Evan's tenacity. "Oh, I don't know. High school I guess?"

That was the way it was in their relationship. Carly would bridle at Evan's smooth charm, then be reminded of a serious side to him that she was always forgetting.

"So, the hair clip," Evan said. "It's old?"

"What are you getting at?"

"Your magazine is all about fashion and chic trends. You must have picked up a lot. What would you say about the girl's clothes?"

"Her clothes?" Carly squinted at the screen without enthusiasm. "Well, it's hard to say. The skirt is a bit long. Kind of retro."

"And the belt?"

"Hmm. Woven elastic, wide."

Once again, Evan zoomed the image for her. The resolution held up pretty well.

Carly blinked. "The belt's a little frayed the way the rubber fibres have broken. They don't make elastic that way anymore. So, the belt has to be old, too." She gave out a little gasp. "Do you think she's gotten her clothes from Lizzie's boxes? Lizzie collects old things—or she did."

"It's a kind of coincidence all right. How about the hairstyle?"

"I don't know. A sort of timeless bob. Not trendy at all."

"Go on."

"What? Nicely combed? Natural reddy-brown, kind of a chestnut? What do you want me to say?"

"If you were fixing your hair like that, what would you have to do to it?"

"Oh, I get it. It looks clean, shampooed, and…the ends are curled up. She's using a curling iron."

"Or curlers."

Carly laughed. "Nobody uses curlers anymore. Especially not a kid her age."

"Okay. But she's not living rough then. And I can't see her holing up in Lizzie's packing crates either."

Carly blinked at Evan's look of concentration. "I keep forgetting that you're not just a pretty face. It's because you're so depressingly handsome."

Evan reached back without turning away from the screen,

holding his hand out to her. "I wouldn't want to depress you. Lucky for you I'm a one-girl guy."

Carly reached up and took his fingertips in her hand. "I'm a *woman*, if you don't mind—always supposing I'm the girl in question."

"Of course you are. Let's keep going. Shoes?"

Carly got to her feet, interested again as Evan advanced the video slowly. "Can't see them very well. You get a glimpse of her feet just before she disappears. Flats for sure, though. Saddle shoes maybe?"

"I don't know what that is, but I take it they're no more up to date than the rest of her outfit."

Carly raised her brows. "Okay, I get it; we have a theme going here. A coincidence maybe, but I'm going to ask Lizzie if there are any vintage clothes in her basement."

"Now, about the words..."

Carly folded her arms in frustration. "But we've *got* no words. Just moving lips."

"I haven't got my head around that yet; there's nothing wrong with the sound on Lizzie's camera. On the recording, I can hear every crinkle and footstep from Lizzie, and her voice is perfectly clear, but nothing from the spook."

Carly held her hands up in tight fists. "God! Don't say that. I hate it!"

"What? Spook?"

"Just... Don't go there."

Evan put the iPad down. "You're still shaken up by your father's suicide. I can understand that."

"It's that, but it's also that if we start getting all speculative and metaphysical about this girl, we'll wind up down the supernatural rabbit hole and get nowhere. What I want is something I can go to Eilert Weiss with. Something solid."

"Still helping your detective close his files, eh?"

"Trying. Mostly I tend to make things worse for him, and I don't want that happening here."

"I've been trying to figure it out with you two. You lost your brilliant father, and there's a void there. Along comes this clever detective who, you say, has a 'gentle' side. I'm thinking—father figure?"

"I'm going to accept that bit of pop psychobabble from you because I've ragged you a lot about your ego and your sexy TV image. I suppose you're entitled to a bit of condescension in return—but just watch your step, bub."

Evan laughed and tried to pull her closer, but Carly was doing her stubborn thing, all folded elbows and pouts. He grinned at her and gestured at the screen again. "Okay. Truce! Let's get back to the words—mimed but not spoken. Let's forget the why, for now, and concentrate on what we can see. We'll watch it again, and this time, I'm going to zoom in on her lips as best I can. I want you to see if you can guess any of the words she's saying. All right?"

Still in a huff, Carly nodded and watched. After another tantalizing run of the file, she said, "I think she said 'I' a couple of times. Also, I can see the little puffing shape we make when we make a 'B' sound."

"But look, there—a puff again, followed by the 'ee' sound stretching of the lips."

Carly stared. Evan was right. You could almost guess what the girl was trying to say. "Yeah, she's exaggerating it, like it's important: 'w-ee-ss.'"

Evan shook his head. "No, her lips are slightly open on the consonant—a 'tuh' sound, or maybe even a 'huh' sound."

"Could she be saying wuh-ee-ss? Weiss?"

Evan turned to her and smirked. "I thought you didn't want to get weird, Car. It's something a little more mundane. And she says 'I' twice, I think." Evan's right brow went up. "Wait a minute! *Twice.* That could be it. She's saying the word 'twice'! 'I…something…*twice!*'"

"Fine, so you're a better lip reader than me." Carly softened, running a hand up to her shoulder.

Evan's look of triumph sagged, too, into a thoughtful frown. "Lip reader? Hmm." He turned to Carly. "I saw a TV show once around Remembrance Day. Someone got the bright idea of getting a forensic lip reader to figure out what troops in the trenches were saying in those old black-and-white silent films. You know, from 1917? The lip reader woman on the show was good. She could even tell that the soldiers had regional accents just from watching their lips. Must have been hard. Those old films can be pretty grainy, but she got a few words. It seemed almost magical to me—her retrieving some precious words uttered a century ago."

"I didn't even know forensic lip reading was a thing."

"I used to do document evaluation for the police, right? Well, forensic lip reading is a profession, just like what I did. We might have to pay her, if I can even track her down, but it would be fun to see what a professional can do with our home invader. The woman wouldn't be too hard to find on the web."

"Maybe the police will pay. If they don't? Well, as long as Dad's books keep selling, I can afford to fund that."

"Okay then. I've got the videos—I'll see what I can do."

CHAPTER TWELVE

The Royal Canadian Legion, Branch 105, was a brick-yellow block of a building with a roofline that owed something to the crenelations of a castle. Three large flags hung at an angle above the glass doorway: a Union Jack, a Canadian maple leaf, and the old colonial Red Ensign with its shield and politically outmoded lions and fleur-de-lis.

Inside, Evan and Carly found themselves in a large banquet hall dominated by folding tables and a raised stage. Around twenty people, mostly couples, were drinking beer or coffee on stackable chairs.

An elderly man with a black jacket full of medal ribbons got up to welcome them.

"I'm looking for Maggie Ross," Evan said. "She said she'd meet us here."

"Maggie? Okay. That's her over there by the coffee urn. Guess you know, she's pretty hard of hearing. Just get her attention and speak clearly. She'll manage. She got hearing damage in Afghanistan, you know. She was a bit too close to a car bomb."

Maggie Ross watched them approach, stirring her coffee with a wooden stick. It was Evan who had set this up, but Carly found herself in the lead, offering her hand to the woman. "Maggie? Carly Rouhl. This is Evan."

Maggie shook Carly's hand, but her eyes were already turning to the tall, good-looking man with the perfect tan.

A thin, severe woman with a tight hair bun and no makeup, Maggie grinned at Evan, and Carly spotted the celebrity recognition thing that Evan enjoyed so much.

"Nice to meet you—in person," Maggie said, smiling as she picked up her purse from the coffee table.

The woman was about fifty, and she wore a tailored blazer over a silk blouse. She had grey slacks and flat black shoes with silver buckles. "Care for a coffee? It's actually not bad."

Carly noticed that her speech was slightly affected by her partial deafness.

They sat apart from the others at one end of a long table beneath some kind of regimental banner, bright with yellows and pale blues. Carly watched as, once again, Evan showed off his easy familiarity, touching the table near Maggie's hand, speaking carefully but without condescension through a friendly smile.

"I thought about what you said, but I can't take money from you," Maggie insisted. "If I'm helping the police or just a sad young girl, then I'm happy to help."

"Did you get a chance to study the files I sent you?"

"Yes, I've been through both recordings." Maggie eased herself back. It must have been hard getting comfortable in the plastic chair. There was nothing soft about her angular body. "The girl seems to be saying exactly the same thing in both, but the last one is the best for our purposes."

"And have you been able to figure out what she's saying?"

"Not a hundred percent, but I've made some progress. This is what I have."

Maggie Ross opened her purse and pulled out a slip of paper, unfolding it and flattening it on the varnished tabletop. It looked like unlined printer paper.

Carly pressed close to Evan, stretching forward to see. Maggie held a corner of the page with one index finger and pointed with the other, her nails blunt but polished. "The girl is saying, 'I tried to stop him.' Then a break. 'I betrayed him twice.' Another break, and then she says, 'Stop him' again. The first two statements were simple declarations. She tried to stop him and then she betrayed him, whoever *he* is. But the second time she says, 'Stop him,' it's an imperative. She's giving a command, or at least she's imploring the listener. 'Stop him!' Then she says, 'Stop' a third time followed by another word with the definite article 'the' and two distinct syllables beginning with an 'S' sound. I'm sorry, I can't be sure about that word."

Carly repeated what Maggie had said. "I tried to stop him. I betrayed him twice? Stop him! Stop the…ss?"

"The last word definitely begins with an 'S.' Just two syllables: There's an S aspirate there clear as day, followed by a short vowel. So it's 'suh' something… Two distinct syllables. Something like 'sultan' but the mouthing of the second consonant is ambiguous. I've been trying to come up with homonyms in English—suburb, southern, summer. Something like that, but nothing yet that makes any sense."

Carly and Evan stared at the sheet of paper with Maggie's precise pencil notations on it. There were sound symbols above the letters that Carly recognized as intended to indicate long or short vowels.

She sat back, mystified. "I suppose the last word could be anything."

Maggie steepled her fingertips. "Well, remember she says, 'I tried to stop him,' then, 'I betrayed him.' So maybe the invocation is to stop someone—a person."

"Presumably the 'him' she's referring to."

Maggie nodded. "I would assume so. But that's speculation,

of course. The trick is explaining that article: 'the.' Perhaps the person in question has a nickname or title, like 'the surfer' or something." She gave a self-mocking laugh. "That's not it, though."

"It is until we get something better, I'm afraid. So, the S-name is somebody she wants to stop."

"Not quite. Be careful. Look who she's addressing. She wants *you* to stop him. Or rather the Lizzie person you told me about. I would think your Lizzie's the one who's the focus here. Ask her if she knows anyone with a nickname or title."

Evan laughed. "I'm looking forward to that conversation, but honestly, you've done very well for us, Maggie. That word—betrayed… It gives us something to go on with."

Maggie Ross folded the paper into quarters again and slid it across to Evan. "I hope you get an answer. You don't need a lip reader to tell you the girl is desperate. She's tired and frustrated. Annoyed, I think. It's hard to watch. I feel for her. Will you be talking about this on your show?"

Evan said nothing for a beat, then glanced at Carly. "No—no. Like you said, we're just helping the police." He accepted the page and slipped it into his shirt pocket.

———

Outside, walking to Evan's car, Carly said, "You hesitated."

"What. You mean about the show?"

"You're thinking about what a great story this would make on your TV show. I can just see you dropping it into the banter while you're flirting with that Siobahn woman."

"I don't flirt with Siobahn. We play off one another." He stopped, making her turn. "Wait…that didn't come out right. Why am I feeling guilty? We're professional broadcasters, Siobhan and I. She's won two screen awards."

"So, it's *professional* flirting."

"And, by the way, she's married to a rock musician, Sam the Slam."

"You made that up."

"Well, it's something like that. They've got a kid."

Carly fell back into step, rounding the car to the passenger side. Evan unlocked her door with his key fob, and she got in. As she was doing up her seat belt she said, "Sam the Slammer. 'Stop the Slammer.'"

Evan laughed, happy to be off the hook, but Carly frowned at him again as he took the wheel. "So, are you going to use Lizzie's story?"

Evan thought for a moment, gripping the gearshift. "No. It wouldn't be fair to Lizzie. Besides, it feels like half a story. I want to see this through."

"Yeah, there's more to this. I just can't imagine what."

He angled his head at her and closed one eye. "So, are *you* going to use the story? As fiction, or…?"

She looked away, back at the Legion Hall with its flags hanging like dish towels under the overcast. "It would make more sense as a story in the magazine. Harriet would love it. Maybe Lizzie wouldn't mind if we used it to promote her inventory."

CHAPTER THIRTEEN

The last one had taken all night.

The man in the disposable overalls worked slowly, carefully, on the woman's corpse. Her name was Alicia, and she had a son and a daughter, and a husband. The man had never met Alicia's family, but she had been talkative and mentioned them.

Mostly the man in the lighted space was absorbed by the other figures there in the OR, sensing rather than seeing them. It was only when a very few would inch into the glow of the big, saucer-shaped light that he imagined he saw feet, ankles, and shins step warily close and into the pool of light. When this happened, the feet were solid, warm with colour, properly shod, and not at all ghostly. They made no sound, and he could smell only the clinical rubber and fresh paint of the room.

One time, he was sure he saw a man's legs and thighs. He could see the weave of the man's slacks and the leather of his loafers, and he was relieved when those feet stepped back into the shadow. He didn't want any men.

No, he was looking for a woman—one woman in particular. The woman who had betrayed him with another man and paid the price. But he wanted her back now. Not as a wife this time but as a captive presence in his life. Someone he could talk to whenever he wished, and she would say back to him whatever he wished her to say. And she would do whatever he wished.

This time there would be no escape into death for her. That had been a mistake. His mistake—he was angry then.

His hand slipped through a slit in his overalls and found his trouser pocket. Inside, his fingers closed on a soft beribboned bundle. It was her hair, his wife's woven braid. He had cut it from her dying body with the same knife he had used to punish her to death.

Death had lost its novelty that night. Even then, he had the presence of mind to cut the braid from the back of her scalp. Now it served as a valuable token. Having it with him, he believed, would guarantee that her spirit would hear his sacrament. He could conjure with it.

Annoyingly though, there appeared to be two women responding to his ritual. One of them had the dark red toenails he remembered on his wife, visible through the open sandals his wife used to love in the old country. This woman gave him hope. This one alone was worth the risk he was taking being here, doing what he was doing, conjuring with death and sacrifice. But neither woman fully revealed herself. Not the one with the dark red pedicure, nor the small almost child-like feet of the other in black and white patent leather.

The small feet of the intrusive girl were just an annoyance. What did this shade have to do with what he was doing, searching for his lost lover? Judging by her slim legs and sophomoric shoes, this was the spirit of some teenage innocent.

Why was this wanderer from the umbral concerning herself with what was happening here—his quest and his near successes? What did his holy conjuring have to do with her?

The Archer made a spitting sound and looked away. All that mattered was the woman in sandals. She was there, just like last time, but once again just hanging in the between place, not committing, not responding to his invocations. It drove him mad, knowing he was so close.

And so, he pressed on. "Et lux perpetua luceat ei."

He still had plenty of time before dawn. He raised the soldering gun, lifting it from its cradle on the instrument tray; the superheated tip had a smell to it, like fresh blood. There were scalpels and drills of every size on the stainless-steel tray, but he knew he mustn't use any of those. Mustn't touch them. He had his own simple tools, the ones he had brought along with him. Even the nitrile gloves he wore were his own.

The soldering iron that he had painstakingly modified for his purpose was hot enough now. He held it with a steady hand just above the corpse's belly and spoke the words he had learned.

He had spent a lifetime in the church, so he knew the Latin, knew the sonorous tones of the priests he had listened to—here in his adopted land and back in Cuba, the home of his youth. He'd found the right books, the forbidden ones, and he believed fervently in the power of the words. Mind you, it wasn't the words that did the magic, he knew; it was his belief in them.

He leaned in over the skin of the woman's thighs and belly, judging the right spot, looking for perfect symmetry, and he lowered the hot iron. With one deliberate movement, he touched the pallid skin and pressed. There was a tiny curl of smoke in the stark light and an acrid smell.

The corpse didn't move, of course, but he imagined he heard a tiny gasp from the watchers deep in the shadows—the curious, afraid to leave their lightless refuge.

He intoned the words again and repeated the pressure, this time on the left side of the woman's belly. Everything had to be done in the correct order, just the way the books said. Sometimes, his sources were contradictory, but they all called for solemnity and dignity. And belief.

There may have been plenty of time, but he was tired. The

women he brought in from the street would come willingly, filled with curiosity and wonder at the place. Each woman would look about and smile at every little detail: the lab full of glass tubes and centrifuges, the wards with their wheeled beds, commode seats, and IV stands—but the pretence, the kindly joviality it took to get each woman here and show her around wore him out.

It was a relief when he got her into the OR. This was the culmination of the tour, and it was here he could give a quick jab to her spine with the stun gun. He did it while she was looking around, entranced by the strangely familiar surroundings, and she would collapse. That made the rest relatively easy, but the simple task of getting the limp body up onto the table was a challenge for someone his age.

At this point, each woman in turn was required to die. Even paralyzed by the stun gun, she would try to resist as he smothered her. The anaesthetic mask was a very efficient way of blocking her breathing, but you had to pack the mask first with a plastic bag filled with cotton. He would remove the bag when he was done, hang the mask on its convenient stand, and no one would know that the life-giving oxygen mask had been used as a murder weapon. The mask belonged here and would be used again by others.

The clean-up afterwards had to be perfect and would take time, but he had planned meticulously, and all the containers were ready in his car—for his tools, for her clothes and jewellery. When he was finished and ready, he would roll the body in the plastic sheet from the operating table and bend it into the old cardboard mattress box. Then he would wiggle the box onto the dolly, so conveniently supplied here in the building by his unwitting hosts.

The mattress had been delivered to him years ago in a compressed roll which expanded to the size of his bed when you cut the plastic wrap open, but he'd recognized even then how much the box resembled a coffin. Just the right size and the fancy advertising graphics on the box made a nice disguise. Even the interior of the box was perfect: a printed cloud scene in black and white with the pixelated graininess of a newspaper photo. It seemed to promise a heaven that he fervently believed in.

The parking lot would be empty at this time of night, just as the building was, and his car was right by the sole entrance door, not far from a waist-high sign. The sign had his name on it. How neat was that?

Time for the removal of the left breast. There wouldn't be much blood. He had waited just long enough for the blood to pool into bruising along her back and buttocks, but he was always careful.

He moved up to the woman's shoulders and got himself into position. When he was ready, he reached over to the tray of instruments on the cart. The knife, though, poised at just the right angle, was his own. It was the same one he had used on his wife five years ago. He had brought it along for this very purpose, and he poised it at just the right angle. He would be careful to wrap the severed flesh up and take it with him in its own container when he left.

He said the words. The right words. Which is to say, the forbidden words. Then he began to cut.

CHAPTER FOURTEEN

Weiss looked up as Prem Joshi came into their shared office. He had a printout that he was holding against his shirtfront in a "guess-what-I-have-here" pose.

"You know that video that Lizzie Collier e-mailed to us, the one with the female intruder in it?"

It was a short game because Weiss knew Joshi had been huddled with the I.T. team most of the morning. "I'm a bit surprised that you're warming up to that little side project."

"You know me: servant to all the people."

Weiss gave him a sceptical eyebrow. "So, what did your facial recognition scan turn up?"

Joshi didn't lose his smug air of victory, holding out the page with his pinkies raised. "You're not going to believe this," he said. "Have a look."

Weiss took the sheet with a smile, ready to give praise where it was due. Getting a match for Lizzie's intruder wouldn't have been simple. The girl was young, unlikely to be on any criminal database, and all Joshi had to work with was a still taken from Lizzie's video.

The I.T. team first had to think about what databases to

search, but, if the girl hadn't got herself into police records, press clippings, or social media, Joshi would have found nothing. Weiss looked at Joshi's sheet of printer paper, and his smile died. The image he was seeing didn't appear to have anything in common with the kid in the video.

"But this is a middle-aged woman. Who is she?"

"What this is," Joshi said with an air of triumph, "is a computer *projection* from the Halton missing persons file. When this showed up in the search, I almost tossed it in the trash, but I got curious how someone so unlike our target had popped up, given our search parameters. To start with, this image I'm showing you is a particular type of artwork, and the search we were doing was based on mathematical vectors. What you're looking at *looks* like a drawing done by hand—but it's actually a tech artist's projection of what the woman in the image would look like if she were alive in 1970. Do you get what I mean?"

Without waiting for an answer, Joshi continued. "Essentially, what the computer guy who rendered this image was doing was an early form of ageing software, aimed at showing the public back in the seventies what the missing girl *would* look like then. The parents were still clinging to the hope that she had simply run off, you see, and they were trying to get the public to help find her. Nowadays, anybody can do this kind of ageing trick using free software. What's interesting from our point of view is, working backward from this artificially aged image, we've got a name. The missing teenager's name was Amy Cousins."

Joshi noted the glazed expression on Weiss's face, so he pressed on. "If the computer artist had done a freehand sketch or even a composite likeness from a catalogue of features the way it used to be done, this likeness wouldn't have turned up, but this is an early use of algorithm software. That means the computer geek took the subject's actual photograph and modified things like jowls and crow's feet around the eyes."

"But..." Weiss said.

"Come on, Eilert. Get with the digital age. The software searches using geometry: precise angles from the corneas to the corners of the lips—that kind of thing, so our modern software down in I.T. looked past all the enhancements and spotted the underlying structure of the girl's face. The software is supposed to look beneath disguises. Get it?"

"Jesus, Prem. Could you get any more complicated? You're saying this aged image—this newspaper clipping—was released to the public back in 1970? And you've matched our staircase girl with that?"

"Yeah. Sweet, huh? It's a friggin' miracle our team made the connection. The image went from the pages of the *Hamilton Spectator* to microfiche, and then it was digitized when all the archives were scanned into the Halton Wentworth database."

"Stop! Stop! I believe you." Weiss looked lost. He read Joshi's careful handwriting across the bottom of the printout. It looked like he had copied some information from a computer screen. "Who is this Amy Cousins? And why 1970?"

"Amy was a cold case in 1970, reported missing back in 1958. But the parents were still alive and still looking for their missing daughter. Back in 1970, what looked like a new lead opened up, so the parents got the Halton Police to revive the case. This speculative image placed in the *Spectator* was part of that initiative. This is what the missing girl would have looked like in 1970—or so they believed. You following this?"

"Okay, I get that. They were hoping somebody would report seeing her all grown up. But the computer sketch didn't help, right?"

"Right. Amy Cousins was never found. No body. No trace. It's been sixty-five years now. The parents are long gone. They never got their closure. Their questions were never answered."

Weiss raised an eyebrow, so Joshi kept to the defence of his discovery. "It's a pretty sophisticated algorithm based on geometry; not like the old days when we used sketch artists, and this comparison—between the girl on the staircase and the middle-aged woman—is an eighty-five percent match. That's pretty good. Amazing, huh? It's like the girl and the woman met in the middle."

"So, in this wild flight of fancy of yours, the girl on the staircase and the woman in the press clipping are this Amy Cousins?" Weiss frowned at the piece of paper in Joshi's hand, thinking. "Let me turn this around. You're saying if I can find the initial report of this Amy Cousins going missing and an original likeness from 1958, it might look like our stair girl."

Joshi wiggled his thick eyebrows, wrestling with the thought. "Well. Yeah. Jeez, this is getting weirder by the minute. If you do track down a photo of the missing girl—and it *is* the girl on the staircase—then what? You want to tell the surviving relatives that their long-missing ancestor has just shown up on the beach strip?" He squeezed his eyes shut. "And she's still nineteen?"

Joshi looked at Weiss's scepticism for a moment, then sat back down with a snorted laugh. "Maybe you should revisit that moment when you decided *not* to throw the image in the trash, Prem."

Joshi grinned. "I know. I know. But it's such fun."

"Well, enjoy your giggles at the taxpayer's expense, but we can't tell anybody about all this. We'd be laughingstocks. No, *you'd* be a laughingstock. I'd tell everybody you went rogue. This whole thing, it's a wholly irrational conclusion."

Joshi gave a sinister smile. "You'd never get away with pinning this on me. You're the one who has a rep for weird cases. How do you think we got assigned this Lizzie Collier business in the first place?" Joshi let his head sag backwards until he was staring at the fluorescent lights. His smile faded. "My God. Here we go again. Another case where absolutely nothing adds up. It's that Rouhl woman. I know it is."

"Come on, Prem. Lizzie contacted the police long before Carly was involved."

"Maybe. But involving Carly Rouhl was a mistake. She… She takes a nice, tidy mystery and spins it off into a procedural train wreck. Here we are with ghosts and ghoulies again."

"You're blaming Carly? You should hear yourself. And you say *I'm* getting weird."

Joshi stared at him, sputtering. "It's not that I don't *like* the woman. It's just… She seems to be living on the edge of the real world. Not quite in it, if you know what I mean." He made a silent appeal with his hands, then shrank back into his desk chair.

"I fail to see how your little morning party down in I.T. has anything to do with Carly Rouhl." Weiss sniffed.

"Okay, but…" Joshi seemed to deflate even further, waving his hand in surrender.

Weiss watched him without expression for a moment, then turned back to his laptop and started to tap away. "Just suppose," he said, "we were foolish enough to take your digital fantasy to the next step: There would have been contemporary news photos issued when she was first reported missing, right? They wouldn't necessarily be in any database. If we've got the name, Amy Cousins, we can probably find a nineteen-year-old face, even if we have to dig her out of a high school yearbook."

Joshi blinked. "And if we do find a contemporary picture of the girl?"

Weiss stared at him for a moment. "Well, then we…" He sagged his head from side to side. "I have no idea what we'll do then."

———

The office printer was grinding away when Joshi returned with his coffee and Weiss's tea. He handed the tea to Weiss. "Take the bag out while the tea's still liquid," he groused.

Weiss pulled the page from the printer's out tray with one hand and turned to swing the tea bag over the trash with the other. He handed the printer page to Joshi, who sank into his seat warily.

"Okay!" Weiss said. "Success! Meet Amy Cousins as she looked back in 1958." He gestured triumphantly but sounded weary.

Joshi took the page and studied the printout. It was grey, and the text was almost illegible. Once it had been a newspaper clipping, then it too had been a microfiche, and now it was a laser printout. There wasn't much resolution left in the old picture.

"There's your contemporary news clipping," Weiss said. "A copy from a microfiche anyway. The image comes from way before computer databases. 1958: *The Toronto Star*, to be exact."

Joshi squinted at the grainy photograph. "I'm not sure what you want me to say."

"Well, is it her?"

"But it can't be her, right? We both know that. Lizzie's girl is still a kid."

"Look more closely."

Joshi sighed and held the page close to his face. He squinted for a full minute before his brow furrowed and he looked up. "My God. The hairstyle, the hair clip—even the necklace. It's her. Wait. Cancel that, and don't tell anybody I said it. What I mean is… I mean, well, fine, it looks like—"

Weiss finished the sentence. "Lizzie Collier's staircase girl." He let his head droop to one side. "Amy Cousins. But as you so astutely pointed out, it can't be. God! Why am I wasting time with this? We have a serial killer murdering women and we can't get any traction on it."

Exasperated, Weiss leaned back and rested his head on his entwined fingers. "Look, there's more to this. Amy Cousins—or her body—was never found, but two other girls went missing in fifty-eight. The difference is *their* bodies were recovered from the lake, mutilated and violated. The working supposition was that a serial killer was preying on young girls back then, too, right here in Burlington. They never caught him, and the killings stopped, so justice was never done. It was widely believed that Amy was one of his victims. A reasonable conclusion, but with no physical evidence and no body, it was always speculation."

Joshi shrugged. "Kind of interesting, isn't it? In a way, we've wound up with two serial killer cases on the go."

CHAPTER FIFTEEN

Carly was standing at the window of Lizzie's house, looking out over the narrowing end of Lake Ontario. The lake was beaten into a fury of dancing splashes by a thunderstorm that was rumbling across from Hamilton Harbour on its way to New York State. The cool glass in front of Carly was a gentle cascade of rivulets that made a steady dripping sound, and she closed her eyes to listen.

Every now and then there was a delicate rattle as Lizzie worked away in the kitchen preparing a tray of tea and small, crustless sandwiches. As always, there was something old-school about Lizzie. Her notion of hospitality was refined, old-fashioned, and inclined to polite ritual.

They sat in the soft conversation nook, and Lizzie would ask about Carly's life growing up in the rich umbra of her father's literary fame and success. This was the fourth time Carly had visited but the first she'd been without her friend, Harriet. Harriet had excused herself for a date with Corey, an old girl-friend of Carly's from University, and the dynamic with Lizzie felt different this time. Lizzie came across as almost motherly, touching Carly's wrist and listening with wide eyes to her stories of growing up in the Rouhl household.

It was getting late, coming up to seven, but Lizzie had insisted she stay for a bite to eat before heading home. Lizzie had a calm assuredness about her, and Carly found herself wondering how she had been with her wheeler-dealer husband who was always on the search for a bargain that could be resold for profit. Sometimes, Carly realized, people were happily content to stand in the background, smiling, while a spouse or friend joked and schmoozed the guests. People like that could be like small flowers who scintillated when the loud and gaudy bloom beside them was finally picked. Clint was long gone.

There was also something about the warmth of Lizzie's house, filled as it was with the memorabilia of a simpler age, which reminded Carly of her father's office—the office filled with keepsakes where A.L. Rouhl had written all those marvellous books.

As a child, Carly drifted in and out of her father's creative space, drawn by his boozy good nature but bored by the gentle piano music that drifted with relentless tastefulness from the stereo. She surprised herself by remembering that music now. She hadn't thought of those endless jazz riffs, low and gentle, in years.

Here and now, standing against the trickling floor-length window, she could almost imagine her mother—taken from Carly while she was away at college by cancer—happily at work in the kitchen just as Lizzie was now. There had been nothing self-effacing about Carly's mother, though. It had been A.L. Rouhl, the great author, who had been content to smile silently in the warmth of his wife's gregariousness.

Emma Rouhl had been a comparatively simple woman, Carly supposed; who could compete with the internal life of the great A.L. Rouhl? But, like Lizzie the teacher, Carly's mother had been strong and proud. Carly found herself sorry that

Lizzie and Clint had no children and made a mental note to ask her about that. Lizzie would have made a warm and affectionate mother.

The thought made Carly turn towards the gentle sound of bone china cups and saucers with a wistful smile, but the smile died slowly. The delicate piano music that had been tinkling through her memory seemed to drift closer as though by some fancy stereo effect, and Carly had the eerie feeling that it had become real, right there in the room with her.

No, not this room…

It was drifting up the stairwell from the basement. She turned again to follow the sound, and there, standing in the stairwell, her face a small mask of despair, was the intruder.

Carly's mind went into overdrive as she considered what to do—call Lizzie? Raise her camera phone? Call out to the girl?

Instead, she found herself moving very slowly, turning her body to fully face the girl. Now this was real, not a 4K video; after all the speculation and discussion, Carly found she wanted nothing more than to look into the girl's eyes herself—to read the message there that the teenager seemed unable to express. What guilt or fear was making that delicate furrow on the teenager's brow?

The girl was talking again, there on the upper steps of the stairs. Her small, pursed, heart-shaped lips moving, her smooth hand on the railing; she was making the same silent appeal. Carly recognized the mimed shapes of her plea—the same futile words: "I tried to stop him. Twice. Stop him! Stop…" and then the name.

There was no point in putting Lizzie through this again. This time, it was personal: just the girl and Carly.

Thunder rumbled far away over the lake, and the lights flickered momentarily as lightning struck some lonely pylon in the rain.

Carly took a slow step towards the girl, expecting her to bolt down the stairs as she had in the video clips. There was something different, though; the girl had finished her silent appeal, and she was hesitating. It was as if she sensed a special connection with Carly—Carly's wish to help, to make sense of this.

This was no ghost on the stairway. Carly was sure of that. Ghosts were pallid and insubstantial creatures, weren't they? This girl was solid and making desperate eye contact with Carly. Carly took another step, and then the two women were there, standing together: Carly open and encouraging, the girl tense and needy.

In the softest voice she could manage, so quiet that Lizzie would hear nothing, Carly found herself whispering encouragement. "Go on. Keep trying. Tell me. I want to help you."

Carly was astonished that the girl seemed to hear her and respond. Could it be? Was she finally making contact?

Something was new. Carly was making a tenuous bond with this mystery girl. This was no intruder, no prankster, no thief; this was a troubled teenager, silently begging Carly. They were two people determined to communicate, frustrated by some unknowable barrier between them.

Carly took another step, and the two were standing face to face. Carly was never surer that this was a living, breathing human being. Eerily, there was no sound, no scent of fragrance or anxiety—just the steady trickle of rain in the outer darkness and the distant rumble of the storm. The unaccountable piano music died away, leaving Carly wondering if this, at least, she had imagined.

The girl made no move to run down the stairs. Carly thought about the videos she and Evan had studied; by this time, the girl should be disappearing down to the basement landing, but here she was—holding her ground. It was as if the girl felt encouraged by Carly's humanity and felt her need to understand.

Carly shook her head slowly in frustration. "What is it? What burden are you carrying?"

The girl seemed to heave her chest with the weight of her sadness. Her eyes boring into Carly's, she set her lips in a tight line. Then her eyelids suddenly convulsed in pain. It was such a sudden change—something different, something that hadn't happened in the videos—that Carly blinked in surprise.

"What are you..." Carly began, but her words died away as she stared.

On the simple white material of the girl's blouse, a tiny stain appeared below her left shoulder: red and irregular. Rooted to the spot in horror, Carly was compelled to watch as the stain spread. A dark circle, like spilled wine, seemed to ooze outward on her breast, and then, with shocking speed, a drip ran down the linen material in a sharp line to the girl's waist. The blood stopped and pooled along that wide elastic belt.

Carly tore her gaze away from it just long enough to see the pain on the girl's face. She was talking again, miming those same impassioned words, but the pain didn't seem physical. It was as if the horrible badge of blood on the left side of her blouse wasn't a wound at all, but a message.

CHAPTER SIXTEEN

Weiss and Joshi were sitting as close to side by side as the small office would allow. Slightly behind Weiss's right shoulder, Joshi leaned forward to read the screen of Weiss's laptop. The grainy old newspaper looked grey and washed out on the screen.

"It's hard to make sense of this," Weiss said. "It sounds like Amy Cousins had been cautioned for making irresponsible statements to her family and friends. She was having some kind of emotional breakdown—raving, they called it. Eventually, she disappeared. They believed she had run off. She was nineteen, and a pretty girl, so the police didn't go too far in looking for her. It was assumed she'd met someone, eloped maybe."

Joshi frowned his disapproval. "What was Amy telling people back then—before she disappeared? What 'irresponsible statements' was she making?"

"She accused a prominent citizen, a friend of her father's, of being a monster, a sexual predator. Accused him of indecent acts. That's the way they talked back then: euphemisms.Indecent acts could cover anything from rape to murder. Sounds like this supposed abuser was a local bigshot. They couldn't name him in the press, of course. He would have sued. There

122

were threats of libel from the accused man that got as far as appearing in the press, then nothing more."

Joshi gave a cynical smirk. "The bigshot's intimidation tactics worked."

"As far as I can see here, the girl had no real evidence for what she was saying about the guy, and her story was muddled."

"She was just a teenager going through a bad time."

Weiss nodded slowly. "What was really going on, I wonder. Was she being abused herself? They didn't talk about that sort of thing openly in the press back then, especially if the abuser was rich and prominent. Status in the community could be used to smooth over practically anything. And virtually nobody took teenage girls seriously—about anything."

"Any clue who the prominent citizen might be?"

"I've Googled it every which way, but there's nothing much related to Burlington and the time period. There's this: 'Prominent citizen wins Civic Pride Award.'" That was in sixty-six. That's all we've got. Another stab in the dark."

Joshi's chair creaked as he settled back to reach a file on his desk. "What did someone do to become a prominent citizen in Burlington in the fifties and sixties? Politician? Business owner? Lawyer? Doctor?"

Weiss noticed the file in Joshi's hand. "What have you got there?"

"This is a list of persons reported missing around that time. The circled names are the two high school-aged girls missing from Halton around the same time as Amy. The addresses of the girls were both in Burlington and they were both eighteen years old and in what would have been grade thirteen."

"Grade thirteen? Is that a thing?"

"It was then."

"So," Weiss picked it up, "if you count Amy, that's three girls gone missing. Only two bodies were found. No explanation. Back then, girls seldom went on in education after eighteen.

Amy would have been a recent graduate. She would have known the missing girls. Burlington Central was the only high school in town in her day."

"So, I was right," Joshi said. "We're looking at a serial killer back in the fifties."

"Could be. Amy was frightened and vulnerable. Maybe she was number three. It's possible."

"If anybody in law enforcement put all that together at the time, there's no record of it."

"Teenagers missing." Weiss narrowed his eyes and looked out at the three flags hanging above the parking lot. "The victims were at the same high school as Amy around the same time. If Amy did know those girls and they went missing…that would have frightened her."

CHAPTER SEVENTEEN

Lizzie came in from the kitchen carrying a tin Coca-Cola tray. The tray was in mint condition, the enamel bright and creamy. Maybe fifty bucks at auction, and it showed a pretty girl in a cloche hat clutching a Coke bottle and smiling. On the tray were a Brown Betty teapot and two milky-green glass mugs. Lizzie stopped in her tracks when she saw the expression on Carly's face. Slowly she put the tray down on the coffee table and straightened.

There was something about the way Carly was standing, her hands clutched together in an anxious ball. She looked pale, dazed. Carly said nothing at first, swallowing and squeezing her eyes shut.

"She's been back?" Lizzie said. "I didn't hear anything. You should have called. Funny," she went on, seeing the shock on Carly's face. "It doesn't alarm me anymore. If anything, I get annoyed at the girl."

Finding her voice, Carly said, "It was different this time. There was…blood. On her blouse. Lots of it."

"Oh, my God! She's been hurt?"

"The girl didn't seem concerned with the wound—ran her

fingers through the blood as though it was nothing—then she…" Carly shook her head in disbelief. "She walked downstairs. I know I should have followed. It was a perfect opportunity to grab her by the arm and make her sit down with us. I mean, she was right there. I could have touched her so easily. I meant to, but then the blood began running down her blouse. There was so much of it—so deep a red, like port wine, and it flowed so quickly. I can't understand why she didn't pass out from the sudden loss. I… I just froze. It made no sense. There was no tear in her blouse, just these bloody gouts suddenly, as though her ribs had erupted. I didn't know what to do."

"You didn't follow her?"

"I could have stopped her. I remember looking after her, marvelling that there were no drops of blood on the steps beneath her, but I just stood watching her run from the landing into the basement room. She must be down there, Lizzie. She needs help. She'll bleed to death."

"We have to call an ambulance."

Carly nodded, but when Lizzie turned to go, she grasped her elbow. "What if we go down there and she's disappeared again? Same with the police. I have to find her this time, make her stay. She can't go far—not with that terrible wound. Lizzie, I'm going down there, and then I'm going to call Eilert. Eilert Weiss, the detective."

"I don't know, Carly. You look shaken."

"It was," she thought for a moment, "like a gimmick effect in a horror movie. You can laugh at it on a TV screen, but when it happens in front of you…"

Lizzie put her hand on Carly's shoulder. "Detective Weiss talked about the girl as though she were doing some kind of magic trick—not real magic, but illusion. You know, like on a stage in front of a real audience. Maybe this is another bit of showmanship."

Carly thought about that. "It's one way of dealing with the impossible, I suppose—call it an illusion."

Lizzie took a deep breath. "Let's go down together then. I'm not afraid of the girl. I'm starting to think of her as an infuriating niece or something. She radiates helplessness, but she's making a nuisance of herself."

"Helplessness and exasperation—that's what I got. She's as frustrated as we are, trying to communicate without words."

Lizzie stepped forward, the tea tray laid aside and forgotten, but Carly wanted to take the lead. She felt almost like Weiss would have, wanting to protect "a member of the public," as detective Joshi liked to call anyone without police credentials, so she stepped ahead of Lizzie on the stairs and started down.

There seemed no point in moving slowly. The girl had to be there, and, after all, she was just a wounded teenager.

———

The room was empty as Carly had expected it to be, the pile of crates and boxes looming behind the bar, the old player piano angled against the short wall. There was a furnace room to her left, but its door was open and, unlike most of the house, it was relatively empty. Someone could have easily squatted down behind the furnace, but it would have been one of the first places the police looked. It was also easy to check; a brief glance around the back: a couple of new furnace filters and some bottles of distilled water. No one there.

The main room was an open space, despite the odd shelf of intriguing almost-antiques lining the walls. Then there was the piano—an upright, obviously old—squared against the corner of the room. This is where all the merriment had been back in those days: singing, band instruments, maybe Jayne at the piano while someone held her little lapdog. As Carly approached it, some subtle movement caught her eye. Carly jerked her head around, but there was nothing there.

Lizzie went on examining every conceivable hiding place behind stacked chairs and a folding step stool, but Carly bent down looking for the lever under the old keyboard. "These things have two positions, don't they? Manual if you want to play by yourself and automatic if you want to run the paper roll and hear the music recorded on it. Right?"

Lizzie turned to her and blinked in surprise. "Why are we talking about the piano? I never play it these days, but I suppose if you turn on the roll, it should still play." She shook her head. "This is silly. Why is there no blood down here?"

Carly persisted. "Is there any way the piano roll could have been playing when we were upstairs—a few minutes ago?"

"No. Of course not. Someone has to pump the foot pedals to play a piano roll. It's a hydraulic system. Very old. Nobody's bothered with those old piano rolls for decades." Lizzie kept sweeping the room with her gaze, her palms raised in frustration. "I only keep it because of the stories it has to tell. I guess I hoped that someone might come along who appreciated all the celebrities who have sat down and played on it. A musicologist or something. That's just another thing I've never gotten around to dealing with. I guess it's probably all seized up now."

Carly straightened and got back to looking about, staring at the floor tiles, expecting to see blood. She kept glancing at the old pianola, though. In her mind, the girl and the imagined piano music had become confused, and she couldn't let it go.

"You were telling me about how the touring musicians would come here for a place to relax and entertain themselves."

Lizzie had begun to eye the stacked boxes behind the bar, tilting her head this way and that, but she spared Carly a worried glance. "Yes, and to have a drink, don't forget. There was no liquor on Sundays back then, so this was one of the only places you could get a shot of whiskey or gin." Lizzie gestured to the old bar. "That old brass rail isn't just a piece of vintage decor, you know. The guests—singers and instrumentalists— would crowd up against the bar and have a good time. This room used to be packed in those days. Especially by the Black entertainers who couldn't go to the hotels and bars on Brant. They weren't allowed into those—any day of the week."

"But why *here*? Who was the host?"

Lizzie was peering between the big crates. "Shouldn't there be blood on these cardboard boxes? If she's been squeezing her way in…"

"Please, Lizzie."

Exasperated, Lizzie slapped her hips. "Uh… Benjamin, uh, Benjamin…something…was his name. We bought the house from him. He worked for the Brant Inn, and this house was just a short walk along the railway tracks from the Inn. He'd invite folks back and word got around. It would have been fun for him to have the likes of Jimmy Durante and Stan Kenton in his recreation room." She shrugged, happy even now to tell her favourite story. "There must have been some great music performed down here. Except, of course, that they weren't performances; they were just self-delighting fun."

Carly turned and took the few steps to the bar. "Yes, I can imagine…" she said, joining Lizzie. She started to move around the bar and drooped her shoulder against the nearest crate. "There should be blood everywhere."

"Carly, I'm worried about you. You look pale, shaken. And you sound…confused. Could you have been wrong about what you saw? The blood, I mean."

"Confused?" Carly gave a bitter laugh. "You've got that right."

She moved into the cramped space, a little unsteady on her feet, until she could squeeze into the narrow space between the softwood crates and cardboard boxes.

Lizzie watched her, more concerned about Carly than the

girl now. "Detective Weiss managed to edge his way in against the wall over there," she said, pointing.

Carly looked, her arm worming deeper in between the boxes. "I can see it. I can squeeze in here."

Carly was slender and long-limbed, and she found that Weiss had shouldered the largest crates aside just enough that she could step sideways into the space. If she kept moving, she could shoulder her way right through to the back of the stacks. Lizzie watched, pressing a knuckle against her lips as Carly began to insinuate herself deep into the pile.

There was silence now, except for the scraping of cardboard against flooring tiles. One box in. Two boxes and a crate…

Carly looked up at the ceiling with its suspended pasteboard sections. The white sections reflected a little light down at her, but there was no direct illumination, and as she glanced around, she realized that she was now surrounded by stacked boxes higher than her head. The futility of what she was doing hit her and she groaned.

"What am I doing? There should be blood everywhere. The girl just isn't here."

The realization grew: Lizzie was right. Carly had had one of those "events"… a vision. She'd lost control of her imagination again, projecting something onto Lizzie's intruder, making things worse. There had been no blood. Maybe in her mind, she had confused the teenager with Weiss's Archer case. The drama —it was all in her mind.

Carly gave a self-pitying whimper, and her voice seemed muted and baffled. With a rush of fear, she realized that she was feeling disoriented. The air was stale and static, and she remembered that she was surrounded by a jumble of dusty old collectibles: wall plaques and bottles and musical instruments… a dumpster load of mid-century memories. What if she collapsed? Fainted right here? She could picture the paramedics trying to drag her out along the dust-smeared floor.

Determined to give up this nonsense, she twisted as best she could and glanced again at the ceiling. She shook her head, aware of how badly she was confused. The light of the main room seemed to be coming from...that direction. She turned around and started to worm her way again, using her elbows to shunt boxes aside. Of course, they would only go so far until they bumped against one other. It was as if the boxes had shifted behind her, obscuring the bar. She was beginning to perspire from the exertion. Her shuffling went on for a minute more.

Carly took a breath. "Lizzie? Can you shout out? I'm getting a little disoriented in here." But no voice came back. "Lizzie?"

She cursed quietly and shoved again until she found herself not in the clear but against the back wall. Carly touched her forehead. "Man!" she breathed. "I am so screwed up!"

She ran her hands along the panelling of the wall until they came to some vertical moulding—a door frame. Curious, she used the solidity of the wall to knee the crates back enough to uncover the door.

Carly spoke loudly enough that Lizzie should be able to hear: "Did Eilert mention a door? This has to be how she's getting in!"

She wiggled into position so that she could work the door. It was a simple wood-panelled door with an oval knob. With a final jerk of exasperation, Carly turned the knob.

———

And, silently, the door swung in.

With the crates so close, there wasn't room to swing it wide, but she had it partially open now. The crack was just wide enough that she could squeeze her head and shoulders through. Carly peeked upwards and she could make out a few stars and a wisp of low cloud. The cool evening air settled down on her, making inroads into the stuffy basement.

She felt relieved she wasn't going to have to struggle all the way back through the boxes to Lizzie. All she had to do was climb these concrete steps, and she'd be outside in Lizzie's front garden.

The steps were clearly below ground level, which made perfect sense since she was leaving a basement room. The stairway was protected by two masonry block walls that held the soil back, and it was easy to climb with one hand on the cool mortared blocks to her right. She took her time. She didn't want to faint here either, and her head felt stuffed with cotton wool. Maybe the fresh night air would make her feel better. But what had happened to the storm? Why wasn't it raining anymore? This stairwell should be ankle-deep in rainwater.

Rising to the level of the front yard, Carly could look out over Lake Ontario. She noticed a low gibbous moon laying a delicate path of ripples towards her across the water. The sky was strangely clear. Since it was high summer, it wasn't yet dark, but there was just enough night for Venus to prick the evening sky near the moon.

Carly's first thought was to look for the strange girl—this was clearly how she'd been getting in and out of the house. But there was only a well-cared-for garden full of summer flowers and climbing vines. The house itself was behind her under a beard of ivy. Above a low wall, the big picture windows over-looked and reflected the lake. It was a lovely evening, and there was even music drifting across the bay. But it was a brash, tinny music that reminded her of her unsteady state of mind. It sounded like someone had floated the damned pianola out on the lake. Way out there…

Giving up on the girl but convinced she'd solved the mystery of her appearances, Carly followed the flagstone path around the side of the house until she got to the back door, and she found herself at the stone steps up to the footpath—the one that ran behind all the lakefront houses. The music drifting in from the lake puzzled her. It seemed to die in and out with every breath of the summer breeze. She should go in and tell Lizzie the mystery was solved, but she surprised herself by choosing the steps upward.

At the top, she turned again to the lake to see if she could see where the music was coming from. If sound could blur, that's what was happening. Now it sounded like a Glenn Miller tune: that big band stuff sometimes played at nostalgia nights at the veteran's hall. Her gaze ranged out between the bushes and tree trunks towards the moonlit water.

The music was out there, all right. Not a car radio or somebody's playlist. This was too crisp—too attenuated by distance. As she listened, the low-frequency plunk of a stand-up bass seemed to float above the water with the whine of clarinets woven into the gentle night breeze.

Determined to solve this new mystery, Carly took the footpath to her right, thinking she could get a better view of the lake between the bushes, to find herself almost tripping over a solid steel rail. Carly looked down, mystified.

She was on a railway track: tarred sleepers and crushed gravel that curved up to the north. That was where the huge, newly expanded Joseph Brant Hospital was, and the long sweep of Spencer Smith Park along Burlington's waterfront. She couldn't see either of those in the distance because of intruding trees.

———

At first, she was compelled to watch her feet crunching over trackbed gravel that shouldn't be there. Her shoes kicked away stones that made little scurrying sounds as they rolled. At least the sounds around her were becoming clearer, less confused.

As she stepped carefully along the track, she began to see people—lots of people—some passing from behind her, some further on ahead. There were young women with summer shawls tugged on against the night breeze and men with lopsided fedoras. And as she stepped along over creosoted wooden sleepers, she could see why they were gathering. There was a break in the trees up ahead, and everyone—teenagers, older couples, women in long, diaphanous dresses, and men in short-sleeved white shirts—was looking out across the bay at a twinkling array of lights floating in the darkness. There were boats out there: cabin cruisers, yachts, and small open craft, each with pinprick running lights. It was obvious why they were there. It was the music.

She could see it now, a pavilion and deck raised on tall black shafts above the lapping waves of the lake. And there, even at this distance, she could see the dancers; couples swirling on the dance floor with only the stars above them and a stringy ribbon of stratus cloud like a horse's grey mane.

And the band.

If Carly didn't know better, she would have said it was the Glenn Miller Band itself. Maybe under the direction of one of his successors? Miller was shot down in the world war, wasn't he?

The line of bandstands was easily visible in the distance under an arcing bandshell. Thanks to her father's collection of CDs and old vinyl, she even knew the song: "Elmer's Tune."

She stood entranced, just one of the crowd swaying to the music. The gouts of blood on a teenager's blouse forgotten, she realized that she was enjoying herself—at least a part of her. There was that lingering sense of unreality, too; the conviction that she'd lost control of her imagination once more and she was luxuriating in a dream.

And yet everyone was so happy; the night breeze carried the music to them, warm and soft. Carly was almost afraid to close her eyes. At the back of her mind was the nagging truth: this was impossible. The city sometimes set up stages in the park for the Sound of Music Festival each summer, but what she was seeing was no prefabricated bandstand. This was a huge building with a wide back deck cantilevered over the lake on wooden stilts. Carly lived practically across the road from the park.

And she knew there was no such building there.

All the same, she was feeling strangely content with the beauty of the night and the joyous sounds from the lake when a girl brushed by right in front of her. She was leading a young man in a brown business suit, his hand gripped fiercely in hers, and they were walking back along the tracks in the direction of Lizzie's house. The couple stood out from the crowd around her —not just because they were moving but because they were intense and serious.

Carly staggered and almost tripped. It was the speed with which she had turned, but it was also because the thinking part of her mind told her that this was why she was here.

She took a couple of long, floating steps and fell in behind them. She had recognized right away the skirt and blouse, the slight frame, the bobbed hair. Carly was maybe ten steps behind her, the girl from Lizzie's stairs—except there was no blood, no anxious expression, no pleading; just a steady regular step as the two of them cleared the sleepers on the track bed.

Carly didn't understand what the couple was talking about, but she picked up on the dynamic quickly. The girl was annoyed, demanding; the man pleading and apologetic. He was a bit taller than average, and he towered over the girl, but Carly had the quick impression of a weedy and ineffectual man. She, on the other hand, came across as a firebrand. The girl suddenly slapped the man's hand away and grabbed his arm as though he were a disobedient schoolboy.

Carly followed the couple. They weren't arguing exactly; it was more a question of her scolding him; he trying to placate her.

"For God's sake! Why can't you be more careful?" she spat.

"But I did it just the way you said…"

Carly stumbled, noticing that they were turning off the tracks, taking steps down from the rail bed, and she understood that this was Lizzie's house. She was back.

Carly eased down the steps after them, kicking a small stone loose as she found her footing. It fell a step and rolled with a tiny clatter.

The two didn't look back. For all the noise she was making, it was as if Carly didn't exist. She still felt lightheaded and didn't want to stumble and fall. She had only the vaguest sense of her feet beneath her. It was almost like floating, levitating over the flagstones, but the tall grass alongside the steps brushed her ankles and the weeds smeared under her shoes. She sank rather than stepped down to Lizzie's garden gate, holding onto the handrail. The bushes rustled by her as she followed the path out around the front of Lizzie's house.

Becoming aware of her breathing, Carly touched her chest and slowed. It gave her time to notice that the music seemed to be fading; she wasn't sure why. But when she rounded the corner of the house, the girl and man were already stepping in through the basement door where Carly had come out.

Struggling to understand what was happening to her, Carly paused at the top of the stairwell. This, she told herself, was why she had come out into the night, to confront the girl who had made a mockery of Lizzie's door locks—at least that's how it was working out. But how could she reconcile this angry, assertive young woman with the anxiety-ridden girl who had repeatedly climbed Lizzie's basement stairs?

"What do you do in a dream?" she asked herself. "You go with it," she answered. "You try to solve the puzzle."

What else could she do? She had been given a chance to confront the mystery girl right in Lizzie's home.

Hurrying now despite her tumbling thoughts, she shuffled

down the concrete stairs, her hand grazing the cool block wall. The two of them had just closed the door in front of her, but Carly immediately took the doorknob and twisted it. The door swung in easily all the way and Carly burst in, expecting to find the young man and the girl shouldering their way into the wall of boxes.

Instead, she found herself blinking out into an empty room. It took her a second or two to get a sense of the space. She was behind Lizzie's bar all right, but the crates and boxes were gone, and she had the irrational thought that she may have had too much to drink. The floor seemed to be moving underneath her feet as though she was on one of those brightly lit cabin cruisers out in the bay, but instead of wading through stacks of Lizzie's unsold inventory, Carly's stagger was taking her on out past the bar—and there was Lizzie's basement room looking much the same.

The pianola was silent, and, with a jolt, Carly saw the young man right there—leaning on it, a surprised look on his face. The room lights were out, but in the faint glow from the small high windows and from the stairs leading up to the living room, Carly could see now that he wore black-rimmed glasses and had light brown hair with a slightly receding hairline. Then he spoke.

"Who's this, Amy?" he said. The young man stood up straight, adjusting the knot of his wide tie, but his attempt at self-confidence was fleeting, spoiled by nervousness, maybe even fear. He repeated the name: "Amy?" his voice anxious and urgent as he looked across the room.

Following his glance, Carly saw the girl.

The girl that the man had called "Amy" was standing there in the shadows, wide-eyed and just as surprised as he. She took an uncertain step, turning to face Carly, and a look of dread tightened her pretty features. Her hand grazed a dark shape behind her, making it swing slightly and creak.

Carly swayed, woozy, trying to take it all in. "Okay…" She gasped. "Time to wake up."

Carly's voice sounded brittle and there was the slightest echo for which she couldn't account. It sounded like acoustic feedback. She closed her eyes, but when they opened again, the man was still slouched in nervous confusion against the pianola. He pushed his glasses up his nose and waited for directions.

A half-whispered voice made her turn back to the girl called Amy. "I didn't mean for you to come here," Amy said. "How did you do it?"

The girl from the stairs looked terrified, but defiant, too.

A moment passed as Carly wondered how to answer.

Carly looked from Amy to the man in the expensive suit and tie. He tugged nervously at his collar. Then the swaying movement in the shadows made Carly look back at Amy. She was standing beside a bloody figure hung from a hook in the ceiling like a gutted deer. Amy backed against the naked figure of a young blond girl suspended by her wrists, and the body began to swing again, gently, from side to side.

At last, sadly, Carly nodded. "I see," she said.

"No! You *don't* understand. I betrayed him—twice."

"Yes, I get it now."

"They wouldn't believe me!"

"Yes. Of course. They wouldn't believe you that this man murdered your friends all by himself, so you stayed with him."

"But I had to."

"Because you loved him?"

Amy shrugged dismissively. "And because if I didn't, I knew I would be next."

"Amy, you *were* next. But that doesn't change things, does it? When he was murdering these girls, you were his accomplice. You're the enabler, Amy, tainted with his guilt."

Amy scowled, her fists closing. "You're not going to tell them about this. You're not going to tell anybody, understand? You were supposed to stop the *surgeon*."

"The surgeon?" As she watched Amy speak the word, Carly suddenly understood that it was the last word the girl had said on the stairs: "Stop the surgeon."

Her mind already overtaxed, Carly struggled with this, but Amy was frowning at the man, nodding at him.

The young man at the pianola straightened again, and his big hands curled like claws.

Carly blinked at his look of smug malevolence. "And you…" she said. "You're the one Lizzie bought the house from. Benjamin."

The man ignored her words, walking slowly—not towards her, but to block off the stairway up to the living room.

Carly shook her head. This dream, this hallucination, this… whatever it was, was supposed to be under her control, and momentarily she would wake up and be free of it. But she didn't feel in control. The girl was. Carly could sense the sheer power of Amy's malevolence: arrogance, entitlement, amorality.

"This is insanity!" Carly shouted. "You can't cover this up anymore. I know what you are—what you both are—what you both *were*."

Amy turned her back with what might have been a sob. The man waited by the stairs, his smile fading.

Carly's mind raced, her hand flat on her brow. "This is crazy! What *happens* here? They find my body behind Lizzie's boxes? Do I just disappear like Amy did?"

She glanced over her shoulder. The door to the garden steps was still there. The madness of fleeing up concrete steps that shouldn't even be there struck her. What lay that way? An out-of-body existence drifting through a muddled vision of the past?

After a hopeless confusion of thoughts tumbled about her head, it was Amy that Carly turned to.

"I know one thing," she said. "You're the key here, Amy. This is your last chance to pick sides. You found the courage to betray him before. This time, he gets found out. This time, they'll believe because it will be me telling the police. His memory will be stained with blood as it should have been all along, but it's you weaving this crazy spell right now, not him. You *brought* me here. It's the only explanation. This whole thing —it's been you all along, running things. So, now, it's up to you. Let me go up the stairs. It's the only way to stop this ugly cycle you're trapped in."

For a long minute, Carly stared at the back of that same white blouse—Amy holding her ground.

Suddenly, Amy's head snapped around and fixed Carly with a stare of pure hatred. Then she glowered at the young man, her fierce eyes flashing anger at him.

Benjamin blinked and seemed to stagger. "Amy?" he said.

And then Benjamin wasn't there anymore.

Carly gasped and tried to reach out to Amy's shoulder, but the white of the girl's blouse seemed to spread across Carly's field of vision like a flicked bed sheet.

CHAPTER EIGHTEEN

Eilert Weiss stood in Lizzie's front garden, looking forlornly at the ground. The storm had passed but raindrops kept sweeping down from the trees and whispering in the bushes. The overcast made everything a variation of deep violet. At his feet, the buried staircase was a muddy shallow puddle between two barely visible rows of mason blocks.

"I didn't spend long on the phone." Weiss sighed. "Carly sounded so shaken I made her give the phone to Lizzie. It was Lizzie I spoke to mostly."

Prem Joshi stood behind Weiss with his back to the windswept lake. The moon had disappeared and what light there was came from the house. "And Carly says she left the house by those stairs?" He eyed the muddy puddle. "Those buried stairs?"

Weiss nodded. "Which is impossible. I get it. I've learned not to simply dismiss what Carly says. She...thinks differently than anyone else I know."

"That's a good definition of crazy."

Weiss frowned and fixed Joshi with a look of disappointment. Joshi tugged his raincoat tight at his neck. "Okay, I'm not saying Carly's crazy, just that some people might think…" He spread his hands. "Look, I'm sorry. What are we supposed to do with this? Aren't we wasting our time coming down here in the middle of the night?"

"It's early evening, and you didn't have to come. I told you that."

"Yeah, yeah. I know what's going on. You think there's something to be learned here."

"Let's just work with it, see where it takes us. Carly had an… experience, and according to Lizzie, Carly saw the girl with blood on her left side." Weiss gestured an appeal with his hands. "Her breast. Prem, I haven't even mentioned the Amazon case to Carly." He shrugged. "Of course, she might have got that detail from the news coverage."

Joshi nodded slowly, saying nothing.

"Look, Prem, I believe we're dealing with a real girl here at Lizzie's house; an intruder, not some ghostly apparition, but… Well, Carly has this way of…I don't know…putting things together in her mind. It's uncanny, but I don't think her so-called visions are entirely imaginary. It's like she integrates information at a subconscious level, and she gets into this state of mind where it comes to the surface."

"You're saying she doesn't know the difference between imagination and reality."

Weiss turned away in exasperation. "Maybe at times she *doesn't*, but it wouldn't be the first time she's steered us in the right direction."

Joshi could have pressed his scepticism, but he just shrugged. "Let's go in and hear what she has to say firsthand."

Weiss gave a small smile of gratitude which was all but lost under his moustache, but his eyes crinkled in a way that Joshi had learned to read.

———

They rounded the corner of the house and stood at the back door. Joshi was about to knock, but the door opened, and Lizzie stood there smiling.

"I've been watching you two in the front yard. I don't think you've been admiring my flowers, which is a shame. I've put a lot of effort into those flower beds."

"It's too dark to really appreciate them."

Joshi rolled his eyes. "Actually, we were studying a patch of mud. Eilert was really getting into it."

Lizzie laughed. "Carly's in here. Go easy on her. She's still a little upset."

Weiss winced. "She just collapsed against the bar downstairs?"

"Not collapsed exactly. She'd been in amid the boxes and when she squeezed her way out, she just sort of…sagged against the back of the bar, knocked a bottle down. Nothing serious, but she was pale and a bit dizzy, I think."

Weiss glanced at Joshi and headed off his question. "Carly hadn't been drinking."

"Oh, no. Of course not," Lizzie said. "We were about to have tea when that girl showed up again. I didn't see her this time but after what Carly told me, we decided to go down after her. Carly tried to go into the crates and boxes after the girl. She thought there must be a trail of blood from the wound she saw, but there was nothing."

They found Carly sitting comfortably in the living room with her back against dark windows that reflected the bright warmth of the room.

They all found seats, Weiss and Joshi nodding a greeting as they settled into Lizzie's mid-century modern chairs.

Weiss smiled his sympathy. "You sounded almost as though you were in shock when we spoke on the phone."

"I guess I did." Carly nodded at Lizzie. "Lizzie has been babying me. I'd understand if she didn't invite me back."

Lizzie laughed again. "Nonsense. You're now my favourite neighbour; certainly the most colourful, and you're welcome anytime."

Weiss didn't have to ask any questions. Carly became serious and leaned forward, clasping her hands. "Look, I know how this works. I'm not going to tell you a story about walking out onto railroad tracks that just aren't there. I don't need your belief. What I need is for you to understand what I'm remembering. What do you make of it? Well, that's up to you.

"The girl on the staircase is flesh and blood, and she's been trying all along to tell us something—something that's important to her and to us." Carly looked down at her hands. "I say she's flesh and blood, but she's..."

Carly rolled her eyes and sighed. "Never mind. Let me just give you what's important. There was a man: young, in his twenties I'd say, sandy-haired, slightly balding at the temples and wearing thick glasses. What I'm describing—it must have happened in the late fifties. The man kind of reminded me of Buddy Holly, except for the hair colour. He looked prosperous and successful. You can pick up a lot from people just from their expressions and body language. He and the girl spoke. I didn't catch much of what was said, but I started to put two and two together and got a sense of what was going on. This guy, he would use his wealth and charisma to lead young girls here, to Lizzie's house. He was young, but he was successful, and it was *his* house back then, see? Despite his youth, I think he must have been someone fairly important. He was well off, well dressed, with polished shoes and a conservative necktie."

Lizzie stared. "You're saying he brought girls to this house? Why?"

Carly shook her head sadly. "They came from the direction of the hospital. Where the hospital is now, I mean." Carly paused and looked Weiss in the eye. Weiss kept his face neutral and waited. "Of course, in the fifties, there was nothing much up there but the old Brant Inn," Carly went on.

Weiss frowned at the mention of the Inn. He had the sense that Carly was asking him to read between the lines. Why had she mentioned the Inn, a relic of Burlington's history?

"The Brant Inn? There's a museum up there now. I've been inside; they have a whole room devoted to the Brant Inn years."

Joshi looked from Carly to Weiss, mystified. "Forget the Brant Inn. Who is this person you're describing in detail?"

Carly returned Joshi's stare, answering in a soft, measured voice. "His name? Well, now, that wouldn't be so hard to find out if I'm right. If this *was* his house."

Lizzie's shoulders were high with excitement. "His house? Clint and I, we bought the house from a man in his fifties. He was living here on his own, and he had let it get pretty run down. That's why we got it for a good price. Clint couldn't resist a good deal. The man's name was..." She thought for a moment. "Benjamin. Benjamin...Morgan!"

Carly straightened. "Then that's him."

The name just lay there for a moment, no one wanting to ask the obvious question. At last, Joshi found a way out. "Did this man—the one who led the girls here... Did he harm them?"

Closing her eyes at the memory, Carly nodded. "I know he tortured and killed a blond girl in her teens. I'm guessing she wasn't the first."

Struggling to follow, Weiss rubbed his temple. "And what does this have to do with the girl from the stairs?"

"I think that the girl on the stairs was his third victim."

"Carly..." Weiss spoke quietly as though this had become a private discourse between him and Carly. "Come on, Carly, how can you—" But he stopped, took a breath, and spread his hands. "Do you know the girl's name?"

"Not her last name. But Benjamin called her Amy."

Something like an electric shock went through the room. Weiss straightened and stared at Carly.

Joshi's big eyes went wide for a moment before he allowed himself to sag back in his chair with a quiet, "Woah." After a moment, he shot a glance at Weiss. "Eilert, don't..."

Weiss forced himself to settle and then gave a swift nod at Joshi. He appeared to want to say something but kept silent until at last he made a weak gesture with his hand. "But you just said the girl on the stairs was flesh and blood. You've seen the videos."

Carly seemed disappointed. "I'm tired, Eilert. I can only give you what I believe. You can dismiss it if you have to."

Weiss thought for a moment. "When you phoned me, you said you saw blood. Where did that idea come from?"

"I'm not writing a story here, Eilert. I *saw* it. The blood was at least as real as the girl on Lizzie's video file. I saw blood on her blouse. She was standing there on the stairs, and a terrible wound seemed to open on her left breast right in front of my eyes. That's what shook me. This was no bullet hole or knife wound; it was a massive stain the size of a saucer—right here." Carly clutched her breast.

Weiss stroked his forehead, trying to compartmentalize. He didn't know what to make of Carly's speculations, but here was something he couldn't brush off. "Carly, have you been reading about..." He winced at the name: "The Archer murders?"

Carly blinked in surprise. "I, uh, I've read something...but not much. I don't pay as much attention to the news as I did when I was a journalist. I never made the connection, but now that you say that..."

Weiss looked at Joshi's shadowed eyes and frowned as though reminding him of his theory about Carly Rouhl's gift. Then he stood. "Can we take you home, Carly?"

Carly seemed startled that the interview was over. There seemed so much more to say. "Oh, uh. My car's here, over on the other side of the walkway, but if Lizzie doesn't mind me leaving it there, I'd rather not drive tonight. Yes, I'll take the ride."

They all thanked Lizzie and made their way up the steps to the walkway. When they got to the top, Carly paused, staring down at the asphalt for a moment. "There used to be a railway track up here, you know," she said, scuffing the flat, even tarmac with her toe.

Weiss looked down at the path. "Really?"

Then they were in the big police cruiser and minutes away from Carly's townhouse facing the lakeshore park, and, beyond that, the great, dark lake.

CHAPTER NINETEEN

Despite the hour, Weiss and Joshi had returned to the precinct office. It was getting near 9 p.m. Joshi was on the phone with his wife, and Weiss was using a map on his computer. He had thought about sharing with Carly what he knew about a girl named Amy. Prem's warning made him pause. And Prem was right, of course.

They were police officers, and they couldn't afford to muddy their methodical pursuit of a real murderer with Lizzie's home invader—and Carly's speculations. Even as he had sat there looking at Carly, the prospect of explaining their time-wasting research made him feel weak. Worse, it would be irresponsible right now.

Weiss knew better than to dismiss Carly's story outright, though. There might be something in the paradox of Amy Cousins, but, at best, it was a distraction from his primary duty. Women were being murdered, and he had only the vaguest sense that their investigation was getting closer to the killer. This wasn't the first long night he and Joshi had put in following what little hard evidence they had.

He had been through an inventory, provided by the families,

of the jewellery the victims had been wearing, looking for anything valuable enough to pawn or post online. Now he was reviewing the locations of charity drop-off bins, speculating where the women's clothes would have been disposed of. Nothing had ever turned up; no shoes, underwear... He was even wondering, idly, if the clothes were what this was all about. Stranger things had driven twisted predators.

His mind was in a sordid place when his phone diddled away on his desktop. He made a mental note to change his ringtones. They sounded altogether too merry.

"Detective Weiss?" a man's voice asked.

"Who is this?"

"I'm Chris Prescott. I'm Delana Brazos's partner."

Weiss was taken aback for a second. Barnabé had inferred Delana was unmarried. The stereotype in his imagination shifted slightly. "Her husband?"

"We're not married."

"Oh. Okay. How can I help you?"

"Look, I know Delana was talking to you. I was sort of half listening in the background, and she explained afterwards that you were working on the case of the murdered women from the church."

"That's right."

"Look, normally, I wouldn't get all worried like this. It may be silly calling you so soon but with a killer out there... Delana had her phone on speaker when you spoke to her earlier, and I picked up on how serious this was for the women of the church. The thing is, I can't reach Delana right now. She's not answering her phone, and she should have been home ages ago. It's not like her to stay out late without calling."

———

Just over ten minutes later, Chris Prescott let them into a two-story house. The detached home was on a corner, only a short walk from the commercially zoned main street with its shops and restaurants. There was a sign out front with a stylized book and quill and the one word, Brazos, curving above—a tasteful sign the neighbours wouldn't object to.

Weiss and Joshi were surprised to find themselves stepping into what amounted to a bookshop. Set up on the main floor of a house that fitted perfectly into the neighbourhood, the shop's shelves were packed with Spanish language books—everything from non-fiction to children's books and young adult novels.

With his balding reddish hair and slightly freckled skin, Chris didn't appear to be of Latino descent himself. Worry was making him docile and withdrawn, but he was as tall as Weiss, and his handshake was firm. He led them through what appeared to be Delana's livelihood to a comfortable living space behind the store.

"So, normally, Delana would have been at home when you arrived around five?" Weiss began, taking in the Ikea furnishings chosen to fit the small room.

"It's a Saturday, so I had just run into work in the afternoon to finish off some things.""You told me on the phone that you got home from work, and you weren't too surprised that she had gone out."

"No, not really. The store is only open three days a week. Most of Delana's business is online these days anyway. What got me thinking was that wherever she'd gone, she didn't take her car. Someone must have picked her up. I thought she might be visiting Addie, our neighbour. They're in one another's houses often enough. Addie's was the first place I checked, of course, but Addie hasn't seen her. If Delana planned to go out with someone… Well, I think she would have mentioned it when we talked on the phone around 2:00. Delana isn't usually a spontaneous person. She's a chronic organizer. She has a number of friends, mostly through the church, and I'm hoping she's with one of them. I've been phoning around, but so far, no luck."

Weiss wasn't sure how seriously to take this, but a quiet alarm had gone off in his mind when Delana's partner called. He stood there in the small, comfortable room asking Chris the sort of big-picture questions that betrayed an investigation without leads and scribbled notes for a few minutes on a flip pad. It depressed Weiss that they had learned so little over the months that this case had been dragging on, and he had begun to see each new victim as a personal failure on his part. He sat in Delana's tasteful, white-walled living room, but he had a few new questions for Chris.

At last, he looked sadly at Joshi and stood. "Let's talk to…" He glanced at his notebook. "Addie. You'd better give me an address."

"I don't know the house number. Let me point out the way. She's just down a couple of doors."

They stood on the porch and Chris pointed at a two-story detached house nestled in well-kept shrubbery. "She's probably home this time of night."

Leaving the police cruiser where it was at the curb, they crossed the street under a gloomy sky without being entirely dark. The daylight lingered this time of year.

The woman who answered the door was small with intense eyes and tightly pinned grey hair. Addie looked East European. Ukrainian, Weiss would have guessed from the slight accent.

Invited in, Weiss looked quickly around a room dominated by—no, beaten into submission—an enormous TV. He wondered if Addie ever sold seats to movies. After the preliminary explanation, he began.

"We're trying to figure out Delana's day. She often spends the day around her house, right?"

"Well, no. That's too simple. We're alike, often out and about."

Noting Addie's cultured voice and self-confidence, Weiss reminded himself that this was an expensive neighbourhood in an expensive town.

"We don't have jobs that tie us down to an office, so we have lunch together quite often; Luk's Diner, Gator Ted's. Other times, Delana, me, and our friend Julie meet at a coffee shop or someplace we can split a blueberry muffin. We'd often talk for an hour or more. Just about our families, COVID, our exercise class, *Parish*, and stuff we saw on the news."

"Parish?"

Addie blinked and then gave a small laugh, tinged with something else. Sadness, perhaps. "Oh, sorry. *Parish General Hospital*. It's just a sort of Thursday night soap on TV. You know, a medical drama set in Louisiana. Now and then, we'd watch it together, or PVR it so we could watch it during the day. It's better when you've got it recorded; we always talk about the characters and have to back up the video so we get all the dialogue. It's amazing how they deliver all that medical lingo so quickly. Have you never seen the show? It's really good."

Addie glanced at Joshi who was sporting a sort of benign scowl that seemed to suit every occasion. "Maybe," she added, "it's...not for everyone."

———

Satisfied that Addie had no idea where Delana might be, Weiss and Joshi walked back up the street.

"You ever seen *Parish*?" Weiss asked.

"What? A medical soap? You're joking, right? My wife likes cop shows."

"I bleed for you. I'm getting a feel for the lives of The Archer's victims, though. They were affluent, contented, comfortable in their daily routines. Whether she's safe or not, Delana's life is part of the pattern. If we understand the women, we might get a sense of what made them careless enough to fall for the killer's line."

From the car, Weiss looked across the lawn at Chris and Delana's front porch. He touched the car door handle to get in, but something made him change his mind and amble up to the front door of the Brazos bookshop once more.

Chris was surprised to see them at the door again. They explained about the TV show.

"Addie mentioned someone called Julie. They'd watch the show together."

"Oh, yeah…" Chris's eyes widened. "Delana'd never miss that show. She'd go on and on about all these doctor characters and their affairs, and I seldom knew what she was talking about. I'd just kind of glaze over and listen…"

Weiss gently urged him into the living room again where a large flat screen was wall-mounted over a shallow chest of drawers. On the chest was a soundbar and a DVD player.

"The most recent airing of the show would have been," Weiss closed his eyes and remembered what Addie had said, "Thursday night. Today is Saturday. Could you see if she recorded the Thursday program?"

"What, *Parish*? I can tell you right now she recorded them all." Chris had to squint through rheumy eyes to call up the recordings screen. His face contorted into a grimace of pain. "Yes. She recorded it. Looks like it's set up to record every day."

Chris hit the play button on the most recent episode and the end credits began to scroll. "She's watched the Thursday show. I don't know why she bothered recording the shows because she almost never missed it on Thursday nights. She loves that damn show. Works her Thursday evenings around it." He shrugged in a sad, burdened way. "Sometimes, she'd rewatch it during the day; I'd call her from work around 2:30 or something, and she'd bawl me out because she had friends over to watch it with her."

"Could you make us a list of her friends—maybe limit it to

people she'd be comfortable taking a car ride with? Oh, and make sure this…uh, Julie is on there. Addie mentioned her."

Chris nodded. "I've tried reaching Julie. I left a couple of messages on her phone."

"The most obvious conclusion is that she went somewhere with a friend or friends. It occurred to me it might be a get-together to watch a recording of her favourite show. It's lame, I know, but it's something we can check up on."

"Phone numbers please," Joshi added softly. "And, uh, maybe you could put a checkmark beside anyone who attends your church."

"One more thing, Mr. Prescott," Weiss added. "Could you lend us a photo of your partner?"

Chris walked to the bay window that looked out onto the street and picked up a framed shot of two people. He handed it over to Weiss. There, in tropical sunshine and framed by palm trees, was Chris Prescott, standing tall and beaming with love. Beside him was Delana Brazos.

Weiss stood with the frame in his hands and stared as the final shreds of his imagined image of Delana Brazos fell away in tatters.

———

They waited for Chris to make his list and take the photo out of its frame. Outside, in the car, waiting for the air conditioning to kick in, Weiss looked over Chris's hastily scribbled list of names. Looking up, he said, "Delana's beautiful. Statuesque. Who knew?"

Joshi took another look at the photo he was holding before laying it on the back seat. "Yeah, but she doesn't fit the profile. She looks like a Swedish movie star—tall, blond, pixie cut…"

"And yet she *does* fit. Dyed hair or not, she's Latina, Catholic, a churchgoer, and she must be in her forties."

"Not a mother. No kids."

"But she's in the circle: part of the St. Teresa congregation, and she works from home, even if her home is a bookshop. Which means she's available… the way the others were available. The way the killer is fishing—finding women who trust him—he can't be too selective. In fact, the vibe I'm getting; he doesn't care if they're attractive. None of the women had been raped. This is about something other than lust: anger, religious faith, satanism?"

There was a purring over the car's speaker system, and Weiss pulled out his phone. Without any preamble, a voice immediately filled the cruiser. "Hello? Detective Weiss?"

"Yes, who…uh…?"

"I'm so sorry. It's Julie, Delana's friend."

Weiss introduced himself and explained about Addie. "You must know Chris Prescott has been trying to reach you."

"Yes, yes! I just noticed his calls and got back to him a few minutes ago. I told him that Delana was with me and Nita after the church meeting, then Delana went off with Nita. I'm sure everything is fine. Chris said I should call you right away."

"So, Delana has been at a meeting."

"Of the executive committee of the church council, yes. It wasn't one of our regularly scheduled meetings, you see. Delana called around everybody at the last minute. Very spur of the moment. It was because of you. Delana wanted us to talk as a group about how we could help the police find the person who's killing members of our congregation. You know, without violating the rights of specific people? We tried, but we seemed to just go around in circles, and it sort of degenerated into a gossip session, so, in the end, we didn't really come up with anything helpful."

"Delana must have got a ride to this meeting. Her car is still in her garage."

"That's right," Julie said. "Nita would have picked her up."

"Carpooling. I got the impression from Chris that it was unusual."

"Ye-es." Julie sounded hesitant. "It's because she and Nita were going somewhere together afterwards. They had a sort of 'appointment.'" She made the word sound like a winking joke.

"Ah. Could you tell us where they were actually going?"

"To meet another friend from the church. That's all they would tell me. There was some giggling and conspiracy going on there. Something about not wanting anyone to get fired. They seemed kind of excited. Just kidding around kind of thing. I just finished telling Chris all about this so he wouldn't worry."

Weiss gazed at his reflection in the windshield. "But you have no idea where they might be?" He closed his eyes. The windshield might as well have been a solid brick wall. At last, Weiss asked, "Julie, are you a fan of the TV show *Parish?*"

"Sure, I guess."

"Chris said Delana sometimes watched the show with friends. You know, a recording…"

"Nah. It wasn't just something like that. They were being too coy about it. Grinning. You ask me, I think they were going drinking. That's the way they were acting."

"You mean like meeting men?"

Julie laughed. "No, no, no! You obviously don't know Nita. I suppose Delana could get away with that sort of thing 'cause she's cute, but she and Chris are happy, so I doubt it."

"But then why didn't she tell Chris where they were going?"

"I couldn't tell you, but they were enjoying the mystery of it, all right. Anyway, like I told Chris, Delana's with Nita, so he needn't worry."

"Has Chris tried Nita's number?"

"He must have if he's all that worried. I told him what I told you."

Weiss looked down at his list. Nita was on it with a number and checkmark. Thanking Julie, Weiss hung up and dialled Nita.

Joshi was behind the wheel watching Weiss's expression growing incrementally more agitated.

The phone purred again until a woman's voice said, "Nita here. I can't pick up right now. Please leave a message."

Joshi rocked slowly in his seat. "So, where does that leave us?"

"It leaves us afloat somewhere in the foggy sea of St. Teresa. What else do we have?"

Joshi thought for a moment. "You said you wanted to talk to the phone tree man in person."

"Barnabé. Right. I got the sense that he had a name for us, but I'm going to keep dialling Nita and Chris. I have a real bad feeling about Delana, even if she is with a friend."

CHAPTER TWENTY

Weiss and Joshi showed up at a detached, seventies-era home on New Street, opposite the Central Library. CJ Barnabé met them at the door, taken aback—not angry or indignant but flustered as though this was the last thing he had expected late on a hot summer's evening.

"It's late. You should have called. I'm about to go out. I'm meeting some people."

"We did call, several times. You've been blocking us. If it happens often enough, we get curious."

Barnabé looked over his shoulder at his small, neat living room for a moment as though checking something, and then stepped away from the door to let them come in. Weiss smelled rum and cigars, but the room was tidy and enhanced with what he thought of as feminine touches: frilled cushions and delicate antimacassars placed on the sofa back. A large tabletop lighter in alligator skin and chrome sat on the glass top of a coffee table, and there was a pedestal ashtray dusted with grey ash. When Weiss's hand strayed to the end table, his fingers grazed a humidor with the word "Dunhill" on the lid.

Barnabé gestured to a chair and watched Weiss settle in. "I

can't imagine why you're here. I told you what little I know on the phone."

"Let me be honest with you, Mr. Barnabé. We're kind of stuck in this investigation. When that happens, we wind up doubling back, looking for new…uh…avenues. Sifting, I call it."

CJ Barnabé had a broad face, a high forehead, and dyed black hair that was straight and glossy. His dark, shadowed eyes and thin lips made Weiss think of a matinee idol gone to seed. He had a hint of effeminacy about him—his gestures, his expressive hands held palms up as though he was perpetually expressing bewilderment.

"So, Pastor Gusmán seems very impressed with you; he says you handle some of the social gatherings for him."

"No, no. Not really. You misunderstand. I'm the contact person, so I hang around on the fringes of things. It's the ladies who do the real work. It's true, I have no family of my own, so my social life, such as it is, centres on the church folk and their families." He shrugged. "I show up for the occasional get-together. I like being around people."

"I'm sorry to hear you have no one yourself. You were married?"

"Oh, I was, but she was taken away from me."

"Taken away?"

"Doesn't matter. She gave me no children, and the rest of my family in Nicaragua died trying to enter the States: my sister, my mother… Heat stroke and asphyxiation in the back of a van. I'm the end of my line, you see, so I rejoice in the Christenings and showers and gift baskets for new mothers—that sort of thing. Just sort of coordinating other people's joy; it keeps me busy."

"I know you're reluctant to point a finger at anybody, but you're in a spot, you see. I think that you were about to give us a name, so now you're either obstructing us or you're about to help us stop a killer. Not much room in the middle. Which will it be?"

Barnabé seemed to get smaller, drooping his shoulders, thinking.

"We were hoping you might tell us if any of the parishioners have been acting oddly—bitterness, jealousy? A single man who is friendly with the women but not so much with their husbands."

"You mean a player?" Barnabé's eyes darted. "A ladies' man?"

"No. I don't think so. Not an obvious Lothario. If he was like that, the women would be wary. Maybe someone who appears harmless, someone the women trust. Someone who lives alone."

"Well..." Barnabé flexed his hands nervously.

"That's what you said on the phone: 'Well.' So go on."

Barnabé cradled his brow, thinking. "They warned me about this, about incriminating our own. We're good people helping one another. Surely, you've considered the racial factor— someone who hates our kind."

"We have. But we have reason to believe the killer may be a Catholic, someone aware of religious symbolism. And then, of course, the killings are, at least in part, sexual in nature. It makes me think the killer is *drawn* to your people, not repelled by them."

Weiss waited, keeping his eyes squarely on Barnabé's face.

"Well, if I were you..." Barnabé's manner became diffident, elaborately casual. "I'd... I'd talk to Hector Lopez." The name came out like a spoken shrug.

"Okay. Tell me about Hector."

"He's not a regular churchgoer. I met him at a barbecue the church held last summer, and we talked. He lost his wife too, so we...commiserated, I guess. Thing is, he's pretty bitter about what happened to his wife. There was something strange about the way she died. I don't remember the details."

Barnabé's fingers ran idly over a side table that was covered by what appeared to be a woven shawl. There were framed photos crowded with the smiling faces of relatives, young and old. Weiss looked for the expected photo of Barnabé's wife, but it wasn't obvious. That made him glance about the room. No wife. No altar to a lost love.

"So, Hector…"

Joshi was watching Weiss's face. It wasn't obvious, but they were both feeling it. This felt like a break.

"Hector has a cigar store on Brant. Runs it all by himself. I see him when I buy my Panetelas. An expensive habit of mine."

"But you said he wasn't a regular churchgoer?"

"That's the thing—I've hardly ever seen him at services or mass, but he'll float into a coffee session or take in a guest speaker. Add it up, and he sort of hovers about the congregation." Barnabé seemed to be warming to the idea. "The ladies know him, all right. He likes the ladies."

———

The detectives were in Barnabé's driveway, passing his SUV, a white Toyota. They stopped at the hood of their cruiser, and Joshi sighed. "Who's driving this time?"

"It's my turn," Weiss said.

Joshi went around and stopped at the passenger door of their big, unmarked Ford. "I was listening to you describe our profile of the killer to Barnabé—the way you put it all together—and I couldn't help noticing."

"What?"

"You were describing *him*. Barnabé. And he knew it. It was a bit awkward actually. Think about it. Pastor Gusmán said Barnabé was a widower. So, I'm thinking, a single man obsessed with his own lack of family and envious of women with family? That could be our guy."

Weiss smiled, conceding the point. "Funny though, I didn't

see any photos that could be his wife. I should have asked him about that." Then he stared off into space over the car top. "Did you notice we're not more than a mile from Lizzie's place right now?" Weiss's voice grew flat and distracted. "Amy Cousins was probably the victim of a serial killer. And Carly says she showed up with a bloody blouse…"

Joshi made a gesture to heaven and then slapped his hands down on the roof of the car. "So *what*? You know I hate that. You're looking for connections where there can't possibly *be* connections."

"Yeah." Weiss grimaced. "Other than that, though, I had something going there."

"Well, don't fucking do it again. It seriously freaks me out."

CHAPTER TWENTY-ONE

They pulled into a metered parking spot on lower Brant. Like many of the upscale fashionable shopfronts that lined the downtown strip, Hector's window was a glass showpiece and a festival of his wares, arrayed like an eternal Christmas display. Incongruously, there were three Harley Davidson motorbikes crowded into two curb parking spaces, gleaming black helmets perched high, as a dare to thieves.

Weiss eyed the window posters showing Cuban street art and classic cars. "I've never smoked. This should be interesting."

"I gave it up years ago. Never got into cigars, although I kind of like the image. You know, Savoie faire, unapologetic masculinity. Funny thing—there's something hot about a woman with a cigar."

"Maybe you'd better keep that insight from your wife."

"I dunno. It may be a domme thing. I knew this girl once—"

"Stop right there. I have to go in there with a straight face."

They got out of the car and tugged at their shirt collars; the humidity pouncing on them. The sun was down, but it was still half-light, the night mist seeming to hold on to the last embers of the sunset. The streetlights began to tint the heavy air of the inversion.

The glass door swung smoothly open, and they plunged into air that was not just cool but noticeably dryer. But it was the dry of a spice cabinet, fragrant and rich. The wall to their right was a complex of cases hermetically sealed with bevelled glass doors. Angled shelves displayed humidors and open boxes of perfectly wrapped cigars and individual aluminium tubes sporting exotic names: Cohibas from Cuba, La Aromas and L'Ateliers from Nicaragua. Weiss scanned the shelves, drawn by the colour and textures. Churchills, Figuarados, Robustos…

The proprietor, presumably the man Barnabé called Hector, slouched behind a glass-topped counter talking to three men in worn denim. One wore chaps like a cowboy, and another had a headscarf knotted behind his long hair. The animated talk stopped as Weiss drew close. The men's smiles retreated behind ragged beards and lip rings, and Hector straightened.

Weiss showed Hector his warrant card and waited with a mild expression as the denim guys lost interest in Hector and shambled past Joshi, making him turn sideways to avoid being jostled. The three went out into the street, somehow making the doorbell sound pissed off. Weiss started to introduce himself, but the sound of big Harleys starting and revving with unnecessary enthusiasm made him stop open-mouthed. He turned and laughed at Joshi, but Joshi just shrugged his jacket straight and ran his tongue under his upper lip in an unreadable expression.

"Hector? Hector Lopez? Nice store. I checked out the prices. Some expensive products on sale."

"You come here to get the best. This is no convenience store."

"Interesting range of clients, though. You sell weed here?"

"You want pot, go up the street."

"Vapes?"

"I'm a traditionalist. You guys got the wrong establishment.

You want to know my clientele? Think wine connoisseurs. Think George Jonas sipping old bourbon, think Arnie Schwarzenegger in the governor's mansion."

Weiss raised his eyebrows, impressed. "You must be proud. You lost your wife, and it was hard on you, but you kept your head and built your business. Do you mind telling me what happened to her?"

Hector frowned, wondering where this was going. "She was mugged when we were back visiting family in Honduras." He waited.

Weiss winced with genuine sympathy. "I'm sorry."

Hector gave a brief snort of scepticism, but the pain behind his eyes wouldn't be denied. "They got her money, her credit card, and car keys, and left her alive standing in a parking lot. They had taken her phone and her car. It was a fucking rental. So, she was stuck there on the sidewalk looking for a cop." He said the last word jutting his chin at Weiss and Joshi with equal contempt.

"They left her alive, you say?"

"Yeah. They mustn't have got five minutes away and then… Then they *came back*. They fucking came back and shot her in the street."

Weiss stared. "Jesus. What were they thinking?"

"You think I haven't asked myself that a million times? They had her credit card and they didn't want her cancelling it too soon? Didn't want her to identify them? The point is, they were too stupid to think of that when they had her at gunpoint. She must have been terrified and alone, thinking she'd escaped with her life. There you have it—my wife was killed by stupid assholes. Stupid small-time local amateur assholes who were making things up as they went." He was glaring now, angered equally, it seemed, by the madness of life and the presence of two detectives in his immaculate, respectable shop.

"I'd be furious—with the cops, with the country, with life…"

"The fuckers were never caught. The police told me that there were just too many gangs operating in the town." Hector tossed his head in the direction of Brant Street outside his window. "It could happen here, you know. It's *gonna* happen here. You guys are losing control of the streets, and you know it. I used to think this country was different. Law and order. Peaceful neighbourhoods." He gave a mirthless laugh and slumped back against a shelf of leather and marble accessories.

"Have you experienced any incidents yourself here in Burlington? Break-ins? Vandalism?"

Hector Lopez looked at Weiss in scorn. "Not yet. Go collect your medals, guys, but it's just a matter of time."

"You got a firearm back there?"

"This is Canada. Only the bad guys got guns."

———

Weiss and Joshi left beneath the jingling bell, doused by the humid night air as they stood on the sidewalk. Tourists and kids in shorts and tees rushed by, enjoying the warm twilight.

Joshi rubbed the back of his neck. "Barnabé's right. Hector is angry enough."

Weiss grimaced at the passing cars and shook his head. "This is too slow. Another woman's going to die. So, maybe this guy Hector has anger issues. Why take them out on women like his wife? She was the victim."

Joshi nodded. "You're right. We need someone who was *wronged* by a woman. A guy with anger issues against middle-aged women: wives, mothers…"

Weiss glanced at him. "What happened to Barnabé's wife?"

"You didn't ask him."

"Shit. We have to go back."

———

They took the cruiser up Brant and along New Street, past the Central Library complex, with its arena and marching band rehearsal hall. Barnabé's bungalow was dark now, the carport empty.

Weiss went up to the door and knocked, knowing the house was unoccupied. At least the gesture gave him time to think.

Joshi was standing by the open door of the cruiser. "CJ said he was going out to meet people, remember?"

Weiss took out his phone and checked the contacts. He dialled, waiting. "Barnabé's not answering his phone again." It was summer, and the days were long, but the overcast was adding to the gloom of evening. "We should go home," Weiss sighed. "Call on him tomorrow early. I don't remember the last time I ate."

"It was lunch at Tim's. You had a BLT."

"Right. So, home?"

Weiss waited, expecting Joshi to grunt in relief and agree. It had been a long day. But instead, he held Weiss's gaze.

"What?"

"I'm feeling it. Why is my sphincter tight as a fist right now?" Joshi said.

"You should really talk to a proctologist about that, but maybe you're getting the same vibes as me."

Weiss looked up at the empty house. It had started to rain lightly, and the windows were spotted with drops that caught the streetlight. "We could be close." He turned and rubbed his temples, staring at the oil-stained asphalt of Barnabé's driveway. "If we're going to corner him tomorrow, we need to find out where he works—the actual location."

"The business card the pastor gave us says he's a property manager." Joshi fished a small notebook out of his jacket and pulled the card. "The number's the same as his cell phone, but there's an address for the company. They're in Dundas."

"Seems crazy to go there now. It's late."

Joshi slumped against the cruiser and folded his arms. "I can't help thinking of all the time we've put in getting nowhere. I say let's keep the momentum."

———

Bathurst Holdings was part of a small office block on the main street of Dundas. It was an older building, fifties maybe, that had been renovated with big windows and glass doors. They spotted a night guard sitting in a pool of light behind a bank of video monitors and she let them in. Incongruously, the small-boned, uniformed woman was wearing a belt holster, and she had a casual hand on it as she opened the door. She was tall but stooped, and her short hair was pinned back to one side.

"Are you with a private security firm, or do you work for Bathurst?" Weiss asked her.

"I was hired by Mr. Fleming himself," she said, taking in Weiss's credentials.

"Can you tell me about the company?"

"It's a property ownership thing. They make their money by renting out space in their properties. "

"How many properties are we talking about?"

She looked surprised by the question. "I don't know. Some of the warehouses and plazas are jointly owned with other companies."

"Do you have a list of the properties here?"

She worked her mouth, thinking about what it meant that a couple of worried-looking detectives were asking questions at this time of night.

"Do you know CJ Barnabé?" Weiss persisted.

"Sure. He's one of their managers."

"You know him well?"

She looked from Weiss to Joshi, picking up on the tension. She straightened and then reached over a monitor to pick up a business card. "I don't know what this is about, but I'd be a hell of a lot more comfortable if you talked to Mr. Fleming. I'm a frigging security guard, okay? Mr. Fleming is the boss. CEO or something."

———

They stepped back out into the brightly lit street nestled in the Dundas Valley, Weiss already working his contact list. Joshi opened the driver's side door of the cruiser while Weiss talked into his phone.

After a minute, Weiss swung in beside Joshi and started punching an address into the GPS. "I spoke to Fleming, and he's agreed to speak to us. He's at home and he's given me the address."

Joshi looked at the dashboard map, then pulled out and drove south on the main street of the town of Dundas, knowing it led directly down from the valley into Hamilton.

It grew darker as they left the lights of downtown and followed the highway. They were in a stretch of shadow between light standards when Weiss's phone rang. He looked at the screen with a puzzled frown and answered.

The voice was unfamiliar, halting and stressed. "You're the detective, right?" a woman's voice said. "The one who spoke to Chris Prescott? He gave me this number."

CHAPTER TWENTY-TWO

"I'm sorry. Who are you?"

"Oh, I'm Nita. I heard about you at the emergency meeting at the church. It's kind of a big deal when a detective questions the congregation. Delana was talking about you. She was spooked about the killings, but she was also worried that the police were getting suspicious of our church members. That was what the meeting was about—finding a way to help your investigation. It *is* about the murders, isn't it? Chris told me you were trying to locate Delana again."

"Thank goodness you called. It's after ten now. Do you know where Delana Brazos is?"

"Actually, I do, and there's nothing to worry about. I wanted to reassure you. She's with a friend. I told Chris as much."

Weiss closed his eyes. "I appreciate you calling, Nita. We were getting worried."

"I'm sorry I didn't answer your calls earlier. I was at a particularly noisy party. They can be so loud these days, what with sound systems and all. These people have a gizmo they can just talk to. 'Play a Latin mix,' and the internet gives them what they want. Amazing."

Weiss released a slow breath and visibly relaxed. "I wouldn't know. It's been a long time since I was at a party. Weren't you supposed to be going somewhere together, you and Delana?"

"Yes, the party was a last-minute thing, just like the meeting, but it was a rare chance to see my sister and brother-in-law. They're just passing through Oakville on their way to Toronto. Really, the party just sort of happened. I got a call about it just as we were leaving the special meeting, and I told Delana that I felt I should be there. Delana was really good about it; she said she would go on without me, so I took her and dropped her off where we were supposed to meet our friend: at a plaza in Aldershot."

Weiss leaned back against the headrest, his eyes widening. "So...now it's just Delana and the friend? May I ask who the friend is?"

"Oh, ah. You wouldn't know the person anyway, so if you don't mind..."

"Something about someone losing a job?"

"Who told you that?"

"Please, Nita. I need to put the matter to rest."

"You don't understand. He's doing us a huge favour at the risk of losing his position."

"Delana's with a man?"

"It's not like that. He's a very gentle man, a bit effeminate really, and one of our own congregation. At any rate, you've nothing to worry about. Oh, God. I've said too much. We promised to keep it quiet, you see."

"Nita, I'm sorry to be blunt, but someone is targeting members of your church and right now, your friend Delana is alone with someone her partner doesn't know. You need to tell us who that is."

"You don't understand. This friend is doing us a favour even though his job could be on the line. But there's nothing to worry about. He's on our executive committee."

"Is this friend CJ Barnabé?"

"You know CJ?"

"Listen to me, Nita. If Delana is with CJ right now, I need to know where they are."

Nita gasped at Weiss's sudden change of tone. "Oh, God. How did I get stuck in this position? CJ—he's taking her to a sort of warehouse building. It's being used as a TV studio."

"Where is this studio, the place he's taking her?"

"Gosh, I don't know. We were told to meet him at the East-gate Plaza, and he would drive us there in his car. He said we could leave my car at the plaza for a couple of hours, so what I did was drop Delana there. It's so we wouldn't attract attention at the studio, you see. Makes perfect sense. It's a big deal getting inside the studio."

"Why is it a big deal? What's so special about this studio?"

Nita sounded surprised, as though Weiss had missed the key point. "It's where they make *Parish General*."

"*Parish…*"

"Don't you watch it? Everyone I know does, and what makes it extra special is the show's in its last season. You see, it's been cancelled! Can you *believe* it? After nine seasons? The network must be insane. All those stars, all those awards? And the crazy thing is, none of us knew it was being filmed right next door in Hamilton. Turns out there are a few TV studios in Hamilton. They shoot the *Good Witch* there, *Handmaid's Tale*… Hallmark movies… So, we were just thrilled when CJ said he could get us on the set. We just had to promise to keep it quiet because he wasn't supposed to bring the public in. Besides, if the word got out, every fan in town would want to go. As it is, CJ has gotten at least a dozen of us in."

"He's taken a dozen of your people to this place? Were they all women?"

"Oh, uh, as far as I know. The show's sort of a prime-time soap—but with really great production values and top stars."

Weiss tried to keep the dread out of his voice. "Has he ever taken anyone there alone?"

"I wouldn't know about that, but I've heard from some of the other ladies what a great tour it is. And it's a lot of harmless fun. All he asks is that we not tell anybody but our family what's going on. He could get in serious trouble, and there's no harm in him sharing with his friends."

"Wouldn't someone at the studio tell his boss what he's doing?"

"No, no. This is after hours, you see, and he's not connected to the production company. There's no one there. He has a key. It looks like a credit card, but it gets him in everywhere. He's responsible for the building—the whole warehouse. He seemed happy to show it to us. I think he understands how fans of the show get a kick out of seeing the real thing. Well, the real *fake* thing. I mean, it would be great if he could get us in there while the stars are on the set, but that's not allowed."

She sighed. "You get to see their cafeteria and costumes, but no actual cast members. There are trailers along the outside of the building that you can see from the windows, but you can't go out there because he doesn't have access to the makeup trailer and the stars' private dressing rooms; they're technically outside his warehouse, you see. As you can tell, I've already been once, but I'm still hoping to go again before they stop shooting the current season. Time is running out, you see. I can hardly believe it, but this is the end for *Parish*."

———

When the call ended, Weiss sat for a moment watching the windshield being pebbled with light rain, then Joshi checked his mirrors and repeated Nita's words, "Time is running out."

Weiss put his phone down, looking up, when Joshi pulled

over to the side of the road at a gated driveway. Weiss blinked at him in surprise.

"This is getting critical," Joshi said. "I'm starting to see how he could get away with this. He just keeps giving his little impromptu tours. Mostly they go on quietly and the word spreads to a small group."

Weiss nodded. "Every now and then, he gets a single woman to trust him, based on what one of the other women has said. Then he just waits until one of the women gets careless and forgets to inform someone where she's going and who she's with. It wouldn't happen often, but when it does, when someone gets careless, he gets lucky. And Barnabé's ready for them."

Joshi muttered a curse. "Now we know why we find the women's cars parked at seemingly random spots—plazas and parking lots."

Weiss thumped the dash. "Okay. Okay… So, what do we do? We need to find Delana as fast as we can."

"And that means we need to get to that studio."

"Right. We can't reach Barnabé or Delana, so we need to find the bloody studio."

"Fleming…" Joshi offered. "Fleming's the boss. He'll know. We need to get Fleming to tell us where the property is—the studio."

He jammed the gearshift back into drive, and the cruiser blew the gravel of the driveway as it re-entered traffic.

CHAPTER TWENTY-THREE

They buzzed up to Stewart Fleming in a towering condo overlooking Hamilton Harbour. The ride up to the twentieth floor was interminable, but apparently, it gave Fleming time to pull on a jacket and put on polished shoes. He met them in the corridor, waving them inside his apartment. Fleming was in hospitality mode, offering them a selection of sodas and juices that Weiss paid no attention to.

"I'm sorry Mr. Fleming, but we have no time. The situation is that we can't reach your agent, CJ Barnabé, and we believe he may be at a studio property you own."

Fleming was in his seventies, grey and balding. His immaculately tonsured beard disguised a double chin and managed to look business-like—dapper even. Having the initiative wrested from him, Fleming fell into a dither, managing to introduce Mrs. Eunice Fleming, but gesturing confusion.

"We do have a large property by the harbour." He looked at his wife. "What's it called?" Of course, she had no idea, and the dance of evasion continued. "Can't remember, but there's a list..."

"The name isn't important. Can you get us there?"

"What? Me? I'm upper management. We don't go to the sites. That's what our agents are for."

It was Mrs. Fleming who cut through the posturing. "It's where they shoot the *Parish* show! You took me there. Don't you remember, dear? I met the star. You know, the hunky guy with dimples." She beamed at Weiss. "He was in the *Harry Potter* films, you know."

Fleming looked relieved. "God, I suppose that must be what you're talking about. What about the place?"

"We need to go there now, and we need you to get us in."

"Get you in?"

"You do have some kind of master key, don't you?"

"I don't have much occasion to—"

"Can you get us *in*?"

"Well, I could call one of our agents…"

"There's no time for any of that, Mr. Fleming. If you don't help us immediately, you may cost a woman her life."

Mrs. Fleming knuckled her mouth. "Oh, my God. This isn't about that Archer killer, is it?"

"Don't be silly, Eunice. What have *we* got to do with a serial killer?"

Weiss wished he wore a watch so he could gesture his impatience. "I'll explain in the car. What about a key?"

"My God, man. I can't…" But Fleming could feel the bellow that was about to erupt from Weiss, and Joshi crowded close to get in Fleming's face. "I…uh. I have a card. I could download a specific property onto the card. I suppose that would get me in, but I—"

"Please do that now. We have to be going. And I mean *we*."

Fleming dithered about finding his laptop and plugging in peripherals while Weiss listened to Mrs. Fleming gush about the stars of *Parish*. "Did you hear? They're cancelling the show after this season. That's a big mistake. That leaves a big hole in my Thursday night, I can tell you. Stewart never watches it, even though I watch all his cop shows. He should be thrilled to be talking to a real detective. Do Canadian detectives carry guns? I picture Canadian cops busting into a room, wagging their fingers instead of shooting, but of course…"

Fleming was back, holding a card. "I can't let you have this, so I suppose I have to go with you."

"Will it be dangerous?" Eunice wanted to know.

"Your husband doesn't need to get out of the car."

"Car?" Fleming said. "You mean a police cruiser?"

Fleming's eyes widened, and, for the first time, he smiled. Rain began to spatter the windows.

CHAPTER TWENTY-FOUR

Evan rubbed Carly's lower back and let his forehead bow against the back of her head. She felt his breath riffle her hair. "How are you doing?"

"I'm all right now," Carly said. "Really."

"How are you dealing with the experience? It sounded terrifying."

"What do you mean, dealing with it?"

"I mean, are you doing what Detective Weiss is doing, treating your experience as something halfway between delusion and imagination? I hear you when you say Weiss and Lizzie care about you, but they can't deal with what you saw. They're clinging to the surface of things, so they can't help patronizing you. Fine, that's what they need to do."

He turned her around, his lips tracking the line of her cheekbone until they came close to her own. "But if you say you saw a bandstand on the lakefront, I believe you. Railway tracks on the footpath? Then they were *there*." He watched the way her eyes were searching his shoulder as though seeking sense there.

"That *is* what *you* believe," he said. "Or are you satisfied with the role of a wild-eyed writer?"

Carly flared at Evan's bluntness, pushing away. "Honestly? I'm not sure." But she knew he was firmly on her side.

"I don't feel patronized by Eilert." Carly gave a slight laugh. "I'm not sure about Prem, but whatever those shared glances in Lizzie's living room meant, I trust Eilert not to dismiss me outright. We've been through too much together."

Nurturing a scowl for a minute or two, Carly seemed to deflate and stretched her neck to relax the stressed muscles. "Come to think of it, I could live with the wild-eyed writer image. Half the genius authors I've studied were either emotionally broken, alcoholic, or drug addled. It's a badge of honour in the genius crowd." She crossed her arms. "But, okay— let's say I *did* see our staircase girl with this Benjamin. What do we do about it?"

"That's easy. We identify him. Not just his name. Who was he? What did he do?"

"How do we do that?"

"I'm a researcher—let's start by putting it all together. Look, you've got a really good description of him: tall, balding, glasses, and you say you could recognize him in a crowd. And then, of course, you have a location, maybe even a home address: Lizzie's place."

Carly raised a shoulder. "Lizzie says the house used to belong to someone called Benjamin Morgan. It has to be the same guy."

She looked up at Evan, forgetting for the moment how nice his hands felt on her arms and the way they tended to slip down over her hips. She smirked. "You're forgetting this all happened to the sounds of the Glenn Miller Orchestra floating over the lake from a non-existent bandstand."

"So, this guy is there waiting for us—seventy-odd years ago. Nothing like a little mystery to enliven my research. I think I'll start at the Brant Museum along the road. Hell, it's within walking distance from here." He gestured at her bay window.

"When you think about it, you're living in the heart of old Burlington. There's local history under our asses. If you were to step out on your front porch, you could see the old Brant Inn practically across the road."

"You mean if it was 1960. The place was torn down in the sixties because no one wanted the big bands anymore. It was all rock and roll."

He put up a hand to stop her. "You say you saw this guy walking from the direction of the Inn wearing dress clothes."

Carly looked at the floor, remembering or reimagining—or whatever the hell she thought she was doing. "Well, he was kind of skinny, well dressed, wearing a tie, and his shoes were polished. It wasn't exactly formal wear, but it was pretty slick."

"Not to diminish our vibrant city, but in the fifties and sixties, there wasn't a lot around Burlington. Not much to dress up for. Let's start with the idea that he was either out dancing at the Inn or maybe he was a businessman working there."

"Working there? Why would you think that?"

"Look where he's living—practically next door. He's walking home. Help me out here."

"Okay," Carly said. "But what about her—the girl? She's just a kid; high school age. Up there on the tracks, she looked…angry, and he was following her like a sheep."

"Then she has some kind of power over him. That's sort of at odds with the way she behaved on the staircase. I'd say she was terrified—probably of him."

Carly walked to the window, as though looking at the timeless lake would help her remember. "Benjamin Morgan was a serial killer. I saw the body of a girl in Lizzie's basement, just hanging there in the shadows. We're assuming the Amy we saw in the video wanted Morgan to stop killing, but seeing them together, that's not the feeling I had. Down there in that basement room, she came across as an accomplice—maybe even an instigator."

Evan made a coaxing gesture with his hand. "So...what then?"

"What if I'm right and she wound up being victim number three? It would explain what happened to her. Maybe she knew she wouldn't be able to control him much longer and was finally starting to fear for her life." Carly squeezed her eyes shut. It was eerie the way this felt like plotting one of her stories. "When I confronted her at the end of my experience, there was uncertainty in Amy's eyes."

"Then what happened?"

"I got that sick feeling, and I think I blacked out for a second, but I had the sense that she was letting me go—or letting me wake up. I'm not sure which."

"Okay, let's go back to the video," Evan said, "to the Amy we saw on the stairs."

Carly blinked. "It amazes me how credulous you are. Why aren't you telling me none of this is possible?"

"I'm blinded by love. Shoot me. What about the last word the girl in the video uses—a two-syllable name beginning with 'suh'?"

"Oh. Uh. I forgot about that. How about... Stop the seducer?"

Evan made a buzzer sound. "Mehn! Nope. Seducer's three syllables. Let's assume Maggie, our lip reader, can count syllables." He began to pace, cursing quietly. "Okay, so maybe Amy didn't want us to stop her partner in crime, Benjamin. Let's work on one mystery at a time."

Suddenly, Evan brightened. "Oh, man. This is a piece of cake. We've got a name, an address, and a description. What I need now is a photo of this guy."

"You make it sound like that would be the end of the road. What do we do with a photograph?"

Pointing at her with self-confidence, Evan said, "You go to

Weiss with the photo and say, 'Here! This is the man I saw in Lizzie's basement!'"

"In 1958 or something."

"Uh. Yeah, well, like I said, one mystery at a time. We've got the name and address, a possible connection to the Brant Inn. Then we can let Weiss figure out what Morgan was up to in Lizzie's basement in 1958. You know, back then, the Brant Inn was virtually the only famous place on the stretch from Toronto to Hamilton. They used to broadcast live from there across the whole country." He switched to his TV voice: "'From the shores of beautiful Lake Ontario, we bring you sounds of the Glenn Miller Orchestra.'"

CHAPTER TWENTY-FIVE

The address Fleming came up with was a large warehouse back from the Hamilton dock area. It was located on a more or less circular roadway serving similar businesses: gated storage facilities, industrial packaging, a van line, and the office headquarters of a deli chain. The surrounding commercial spaces were mostly dark, but there was a line of tall pole lights along the circle. One of the parking lots lit up as a motion sensor caught them as they passed.

Joshi pulled into the parking lot indicated by their GPS.

Fleming leaned forward from the back seat and was a little put out when his nose touched a reinforced plastic shield. "Yes! This is it."

They drew close to the building entrance and a small circle of illumination from a security light. There appeared to be only one entrance to the two-story block sheathed in steel panelling. The little glass portico seemed oddly out of scale for the huge hanger-sized building. The single entrance door was set neatly into the corner of the windowless wall.

Fleming shouted through the plastic, "I wouldn't recognize Barnabé's car, but that's his designated parking spot. See the

'Property Manager' sign?" There was a white Toyota Highlander SUV in the spot, and it was the only car in sight. "He must be inside."

"Would there be any legitimate reason for him to be here at this hour?" Weiss asked, staring out at the door.

Fleming sagged back, stroking his chin. "Not really. I mean, technically, he's responsible for the property, and that includes security, but we have a contractor that watches most of the businesses around here at night. They drive around every couple of hours, but they don't go inside unless the alarm system is triggered."

"But Barnabé has access when he wants it. Right?"

"Well, I suppose. He's paid for the responsibility after all." Fleming sounded defensive. "He has a chip card, and that disables the alarm. The same card is programmed to open all the major doors inside."

"Are there any other exits?"

"There's a large garage-style door that accesses a big shipping space inside the building. It's where they take deliveries and such. If I remember correctly, the film company has their trailers just outside there. You know, star dressing rooms, makeup—that sort of thing. The trailers are all locked and only the film people have keys for those."

"Could Barnabé open the garage?"

Fleming thought for a moment. "I honestly don't know. I'll tell you one thing, though; it would make a hell of a racket rolling up."

Weiss looked across at Joshi.

Joshi nodded. "The setup is perfect for him. The damn studio is his personal slaughterhouse."

Fleming winced as his cop-movie imagination ran wild. "Now and then, Barnabé shows potential clients around the various properties he's responsible for." He shook his head. "But the Gateway Production Company—the TV people—their lease expires soon. Like Eunice said, the show's shutting down production soon. They'll have to empty all that space: sets, equipment, computer suites…"

Weiss turned. "Computers?"

Fleming smiled. "Oh, yeah. Everything is run from the computer monitors on the second floor. People think the show is being run from here in Hamilton, but what really happens is that they shoot the scenes here and upload them to L.A. Some producer in the States edits the raw digital files down there. Everything is done digitally now. That's why the cameras can be so small and light. They lock all the equipment away each night. It's actually kind of creepy. With the light stands and cameras gone, the whole place looks just like a hospital in Louisiana."

"Why Louisiana?"

"Gosh, I don't know. Ask the writers. The point is, it's like an abandoned hospital after hours. Spooky as hell."

Weiss and Joshi got out and did a walk around Barnabé's car.

Joshi glanced over the Highlander's roof at Weiss. "Large cardboard box in the back."

Weiss noted the mattress box clearly printed with prancing sheep; its intended contents well marked in blue lettering. He nodded slowly.

Weiss turned back to Fleming who had gotten out of the back seat and was holding onto the rear door. "Mr. Fleming, I'll need that key."

"You don't understand. I'm responsible for that building and everything inside. I can't let this key out of my sight. I'll have to come in with you."

"Try to understand this, Mr. Fleming. Detective Joshi and I are going into that building in the hopes we can save a woman from a deranged serial killer. On balance, it would be a very bad idea to bring a member of the public along. No offence."

"But the liability!"

Weiss held out a hand for the key. "He cuts off a breast and brands their bodies."

"He... Ah, well..." Fleming pulled a small brown envelope from his jacket with painful reluctance and shook out a card the same size as a credit card. "This is essentially the same as the one Barnabé carries."

Weiss took the card. "You have to remain in the car, Mr. Fleming. Keep your phone handy and wait for us to call. Prem, call for a backup cruiser but tell them to stay here in the parking lot. "

Joshi got out his phone. "We're going in alone?"

Weiss stared up at the soaring steel siding. "What else can we do, Prem? The way it's looking, we have to assume Barnabé has Delana in there. Her safety has to be our first concern—so we go in quietly and hope we get to Delana before Barnabé has time to panic and kill her."

Weiss studied the warehouse entrance for a moment, a steel case door inset with reinforced glass, then he slipped Fleming's card into a slot. There was a loud click and they entered. It was a double-door arrangement with a small breezeway between the two glass doors.

The inner door led into a small office space with a desk and a large wall calendar with notations scribbled on each day except for most weekends. Off to their left was an open space filled with dozens of hanging costumes on rolling stands. Some were medical scrubs, but there were glamorous gowns and designer coats there, too. One rack was hung with men's suits of various sizes, the seams marked with dressmaker's chalk.

Weiss stood in the space, looking about the office. There was a desk against the calendar wall. "This side must be for the building manager—Barnabé's company."

Straight ahead was the gloom of the studio area.

"Look, Prem, we're going to have to think this through. If Barnabé's in here, he could flank me and get back to this doorway. You need to stay here and make sure he doesn't get out to his car—or to Fleming. I've got my phone; I'll wear an earpiece and stay in touch with you. If I see him break for the exit, I can warn you. I might have to deal with Delana, so be ready with your sidearm."

Joshi smirked. "Sidearm. It's kinda cute the way you talk about guns, Eilert. I think they embarrass you."

"Just be careful and keep an eye out for the backup guys in the parking lot."

Joshi touched his belt holster. "We could be wrong about this."

Tapping his phone, Weiss said, "I'll be happy if we're wrong and the evening ends with everybody alive and accounted for." He slipped his phone into his jacket and poked an earbud in one ear. "Okay, Prem, you remember how this thing works. The earpiece has a mic built in, and I'm live. Keep listening in."

As Joshi handled his phone, Weiss turned away, starting down a short corridor that took him into the first of the prepared sets, and it was a shock: a huge entrance hall soared up two floors, dominated by tall windows that looked out into a nighttime street scene. At least they looked like windows. In fact, he could tell there was no glass in the floor-to-ceiling frames. It was as if, suddenly, he had stepped into the foyer of a great metropolitan hospital, but he could tell that the convincing street scene framed by the windows was printed on a huge vinyl curtain that seemed to run along the inside wall of the building. The fake windows gave an eerie sense of spaciousness.

Weiss got what Fleming had been talking about: the emptiness felt wrong. There should be people milling about. Instead, there was a creepy quiet which was at odds with what he was seeing.

Despite what Fleming told him, Weiss had imagined that there would be rows of lights mounted on overhead poles, but

Fleming was right. Those days were gone. Modern digital camera equipment was small and portable, and so was the lighting. The net result was a series of sets which looked real, from the ceilings to the floors, unless you looked very closely. There was a wide staircase which could have been marble—until you noticed the skilful paint job. It rose to a landing and turned back on itself towards the second floor. Fleming had said that most of the second story was reserved for the production equipment, like the digital hub which could immediately share daily recordings with Los Angeles.

Weiss knew from talking to Fleming that there were offices up there, and a cafeteria space for the production team and actors on call. There was an outside chance Barnabé would be up there, but Weiss doubted it. The predator would lure his victims with the glamour sets—the familiar scenes they had seen so many times on TV. He craned his neck to the side until he reached the sight line where the illusion ended. The cameras would never see the tubular metal railings and plywood upstairs, or the great aluminium ventilation ducts.

Turning back to the great hall with its reception desk and triage area, he walked silently on his rubber-soled shoes. It was gloomy but not entirely dark. There were unobtrusive security lights high on the walls. When they needed to shoot in here, the lighting director would create believable evening tones or, with a switch of curtains, the street scene would be transformed, bathed in artificial daylight.

Moving quickly, he listened for movement or talk. Barnabé would be showing his victim around, maybe boasting about meeting the stars, chatting about favourite episodes. Weiss kept imagining how this had to work. He knew that the murder weapon was a rubber mask, and he knew that at some point, Barnabé used a knife for the mutilations. There would be blood. How would it be managed and cleaned up?

He left the hall, passing a long ward lined with beds and

partially obscured by hanging privacy curtains. He listened for a moment but figured that Barnabé didn't need privacy. He was all alone in the cavernous spaces. What he needed was a work surface.

Continuing from one illusion to the next, Weiss was abruptly taken aback. He found himself looking at an EMS truck in front of heavy roll-up exit doors.

At first, he thought that this was the receiving garage Fleming had described. There was a bright yellow gurney propped up on its wheeled undercarriage. It took him a few seconds to understand that this was just another scenario; the doors went nowhere, and up close, he could tell the truck had been painted by the set decorator.

There was a sudden bumping sound, and Weiss wheeled around. Heading for the sound, he was nearly running now, his right hand touching his belt holster.

He passed what looked like a bank of two elevators. The door of the left elevator was slightly parted in a way that would have looked peculiar on a real elevator. Stopping, he drew his weapon and used his free hand to pull open the elevator's sliding doors. They slid apart easily, and he waved his gun at the gloomy interior. It was empty, but to one side, just out of sight of a supposed camera, was a blue vinyl rope that ended in a sort of handle. Standing between the doors he reached in and gave the rope a tug. He was surprised when the doors started to close on him.

"Huh," he muttered.

Everything here was an illusion. The elevator went nowhere, and the doors operated on a simple pulley system. It was all about camera angles.

Leaving the left elevator partly open, he moved on down the corridor. Off to his left was an entranceway. He veered into a short passage ending in a porcelain-lined room with sinks. To his right was a large window. This one had actual glass in it, and it had been sprayed with an anti-glare coating so the portable lights wouldn't ruin the shot with unwanted reflections. Human bodies arrayed on wheeled carts were jammed into the space, and someone had tried to stack them two and three deep.

Breathing rapidly, Weiss approached the nearest plastic-swathed corpse and reached out his hand. The plastic rustled and parted so that he could touch the pale skin.

"Jesus…" He gasped. "Rubber!"

The corpses were props. His mind did a sort of flip: one moment he was staring at a hellish morgue. The next, he was in a storage room filled with rubber-covered dummies.

Joshi's voice popped in his ear. "Rubber? Who's got rubber?"

"It's okay, Prem. False alarm. Keep listening in."

Weiss backed out into the main hallway and resumed his careful search. It was clear to him that he was looking for a ventilator mask and that he would find this murder weapon in something resembling an operating room. Logic told him it would be a major set—the place where much of the show's life and death drama took place.

He found what he was looking for, laid out as close to reality as possible.

The arrangement allowed the camera operator to move about and shoot from virtually any direction. Here was the scrub area with its sinks, there were the swinging doors to the operating room itself.

Weiss straightened and listened. There was light on the other side of those doors. Not the feeble glow of the security lighting, but the glare of a fixture. Weiss moved quickly, but as silently as he could, until he could see through the small, rounded windows set into the swinging doors. A glance to the left and a shiver of horror passed through Weiss's chest.

This was it, all right: the operating room set—the one where life and death were communicated to the television viewers by the chirping of bright displays. But he was too late.

Delana's body was slumped face down over a sheet of plastic. Her arms were splayed on the operating table, her feet still touching the floor.

She was wearing a fashionable blue pantsuit, the jacket top distorted by her collapse to expose the small of her back, and her phone was still clasped in her right hand. Delana hadn't used it to call her partner—she'd almost certainly been taking photographs with it when the killer struck.

Weiss slammed through the set of double doors into the OR, and, in that second, two things happened: The slumped blond figure of Delana twitched, and she groaned… and CJ Barnabé stepped into the light.

He was as startled as Weiss, and he still had the stun gun in his hand, black and shaped like an old model cell phone. There was only one bright light illuminating the table. Everywhere else in the space was in gloom.

The whole situation ran through Weiss's head like a time-lapse film. This was how Barnabé did it—waiting until the woman was marvelling over the operating table. If he needed to explain the plastic sheet that was draped over the table, Barnabé would just say it was to protect the crucial set for the cameras. Then a violent shock to the woman's neck and spine.

With a little luck, Barnabé could shove the paralyzed victim right onto the table, aided by the pressure on her neck. He would need to turn her over to get at her mouth and nose, but he didn't even need to lift her legs. He could smother her as she was arched back over the plastic sheeting. The anaesthesia mask was right there, hanging on a chrome hook. All he needed to do was seal it somehow and press it over the woman's face, holding her down.

———

Barnabé started to recover, backing away a step, holding the stun gun in both hands, uncertain what to do. Released from his grip, Delana slipped from the table and sank to the floor, dragging some of the plastic sheeting down with her.

Weiss lunged forward, his first instinct to secure the victim and cradle her slumping head to the floor. In one swift movement, Barnabé bolted into the shadows. It looked like Delana was breathing shallowly, her body continuing to twitch and spasm. Weiss waved his gun, searching the shadows while he was still on one knee, but there was no sign of Barnabé now.

Holstering his weapon, Weiss did a quick assessment of Delana's condition. It wasn't easy in the shadow of the table with the plastic collapsing about her, but he had been trained in the use and consequences of electro-shock weapons so he was reasonably sure she would recover if her air passages were clear. Laying her out carefully on the floor, he touched his earbud.

"Prem? I have Delana. She's alive but debilitated. Stable, I think. Barnabé's fled the scene, but he's in the building."

"Are you okay?" Joshi hissed.

"Fine. I'm going after Barnabé. He'll head for the only exit, and that means you—so be ready to hold him or shoot."

Joshi answered, his voice tiny and distant. "The backup unit is in the parking lot with Fleming now. I've already called for a medical team, but they're not here yet."

"Keep monitoring your phone. I'll tell you when I need support."

"Barnabé may be armed."

"It didn't look like it. I just saw the stun gun. Delana will be safe for now. You can't send the medics in until the building is secure. I'm going to try to get a sense of which way Barnabé went. He may guess that we've got the entrance covered and try to hide. There are plenty of places he could go to ground in here. The place is jammed with sets, backdrops, and cabinets.

We may have to use the second unit for a search but let me see if I can track him first."

Weiss left Delana lying in a tangle of plastic sheeting and pulled his gun again. Leading with his outstretched arm, he slipped into the gloom behind the table. It only took him a dozen steps before the realistic OR set gave way to canvas flats and twisting power cables.

There was a solid outer wall ahead of him dimly lit by the security lighting, and the sheet metal walls looked like part of the building itself. To his right was a secondary wall made of construction-grade timber and plywood. He recognized the shape of the windows; he was looking at the main corridor of the hospital set from behind. There was a doorway in the wall, and it seemed likely that Barnabé would have gone that way.

Once through the door, he found himself back in the illusion of a big city hospital complete with every detail, except people. He could see for quite a distance down the corridor, so he felt safe in running towards the entry hall set with its soaring roof and grand windows looking out on a nighttime street scene.

And there, on the far side of the great hall, was a peculiar sight.

Barnabé was hurrying, not towards the great glass doors of the hospital, but to one of the tall windows to one side. Instead of crashing into a sheet of plate glass, however, he was stepping right through the empty window frame.

As Weiss ran after him, Barnabé, through the window frame now, seemed to be edging along to his left as though walking a narrow ledge. When Weiss got to the window, he understood: the street scene outside was a tall hanging sheet of mylar plastic with the night scene graphic printed on it. Behind it was probably a daytime scene on a separate track.

Weiss raised his gun against the gloom and called out. "All right, CJ. Stop right there. It's dark back here, and if I shoot, I'll probably have to kill you."

Weiss could make out Barnabé's shadow: a black hole in the murk. They were separated by about thirty feet and the mylar scrim was waving gently beside them, disturbed by their motion.

Barnabé stopped and turned to face Weiss. His body seemed to slump, and all that Weiss could make out of his expression was a blank stare. His voice was flat too, governed only by the rhythm of his heavy breathing.

"I'm not too concerned about dying, Detective Weiss."

Weiss remembered the voice: slightly accented, cultured. His conversational tone seemed out of place. This, it seemed, was a man used to being detached from reality.

"I'm actually…kind of curious about death," Barnabé said. "It may sound strange, but I'm thinking death is whatever you believe it to be. If you believe in death as a *thing*, you can manipulate it."

Weiss, panting, was anything but detached. He groaned. "I'm a simple guy, CJ. I'm just thinking about what a lead slug is going to do to your ribcage. This isn't a real hospital, remember—you'll be bleeding your guts out in a damn warehouse."

It wasn't pitch black in the narrow space, but the utility lights were blocked by a wood-framed wall to their left. Behind the hanging scrims, Weiss guessed that the real outer wall of the warehouse was a foot or two away. All that Weiss could see of Barnabé was his outline. With his weapon trained at Barnabé's chest, Weiss was making sure that CJ wasn't raising a weapon of his own, but Barnabé's fists appeared empty and low at his sides.

All the same, something happened—so suddenly, that Weiss nearly fired instinctively. A small flare of light seemed to burst from beneath Barnabé's thumb—a cigar lighter—and instead of winking out, the flame seemed to run straight up the plastic scrim like a slow-motion bolt of lightning.

Barnabé's face suddenly loomed red: a frown touched with a satisfied smile.

Weiss blinked at the spreading fire between them. "What the hell have you done?!"

"It's the mylar. Burns like gasoline, you see." Barnabé gave a bitter laugh. "*Parish General!* Ha! I have a mind to take this whole ridiculous bloody soap opera with me."

His mind jammed with desperate options; Weiss was astounded at the rate the towering photographic street scene was being consumed by a bright sheet of flame. Almost immediately, he felt the impossible sensation of rain falling from an invisible sky. The automatic sprinkler system had turned on, and the flames began to abate as water ran in rivulets down the plastic scrim.

In the fiery chaos, Barnabé had disappeared, and for a moment Weiss imagined that his fugitive had succumbed to the flames, but there was no smouldering heap on the narrow floor. In fact, the scene before him was bizarre. The mylar vista had been eaten away by the flames, exposing part of a realistic daytime scrim, framed in a tall, ragged arch of smoking, blistering night.

His face streaming with water, his jacket soaked through, Weiss shuffled to the spot where Barnabé had stood. The water hissed and trickled around him, and up ahead he could see a shaft of weak light. That meant more window frames looking out onto the scrim.

Some artificial trees had been jammed into the narrow space to provide a foreground for the street scenes, and through their branches, Weiss recognized another corridor inside. There was no glass in any of the windows, so it would have been easy for Barnabé to step through into the corridor set. He knew the whole building well. It was Barnabé's job to manage the property—not the temporary structures inside the warehouse but the building itself.

Stepping through the window, Weiss could see that this was a secondary set, designed to look like another hospital corridor.

A voice in his ear chirped, "What the hell, Eilert? I'm soaked to the skin out here. What's going on?"

"Barnabé tried to set fire to the place. The sprinklers are controlling the fire, but he's still at large. He can't be far. I'm being careful."

Joshi blustered in his ear, but it was mostly disparaging comments about the sprinklers. He could make out the words "Fucking rainstorm" but not much else. Instead, Weiss was scanning every inch of his surroundings over the barrel of his service piece. The corridor widened up ahead, and Weiss recognized it as the bank of elevators he had passed earlier: two square frames with realistic sliding doors in each. Weiss knew these elevators went nowhere, but they could be used as a hiding place.

Barnabé wasn't up ahead, so Weiss took a minute to touch the elevator doors. The right set of doors was closed tightly, but he knew now he could easily slide one of the doors back with his left hand.

The doors on their pulley tracks slid apart. The faithfully reproduced elevator interior was dark but empty.

He tensed when he noticed that the second set of doors was slightly apart. That was the one he had opened earlier—but when he had left it, the doors were open wider…

———

His gun ready, he slipped his fingers around the nearest door and pulled hard.

The door flew aside, and Weiss was hit with a freezing blast of white that blinded him and made him stagger. Out of the blinding cloud, there was a percussive red flash like a spark going off in his brain, and Weiss dropped to the floor, his pistol clattering along the floor tiles.

Barnabé dropped the fire extinguisher and lunged for Weiss's gun. His vision a blur of red mist and his head a storm of pain and confusion, Weiss had just enough awareness to roll into the elevator and slump against its wall.

His hand shot up to the rope with its handle, and he gave it a violent yank. The elevator doors slammed shut, plunging him into a darkness so profound that he could see only the tiny sparks of his damaged nerve endings. Desperate and expecting to die, he hung on the blue rope with all his weight and for a moment, all was silent, except for the rush of the sprinklers.

Then there was a scrabbling sound as though Barnabé was trying to find a grip on the smooth doors of the fake elevator. Weiss hung heavily on the rope with both hands, his head spinning. He knew he was on the edge of passing out and he knew that meant he was about to die. In a daze, he heard Prem Joshi's voice, but he was beyond understanding what his partner was saying. It was like a bee buzzing in his ear.

In the black miasma of his mind, there were four explosive bangs and four angled shafts of light smashed across the small space. Barnabé was shooting the door, trying to kill him. So far, he had missed, but how many more lives did Weiss have?

———

Barnabé looked at the bullet holes in the door and considered pumping another four shots into the elevator. He knew a thing or two about guns, but he wasn't sure how many rounds were left in Weiss's pistol.

CJ Barnabé was armed now, and maybe he could shoot his way out of this bloody parody of a hospital. It was unlikely he'd survive. They probably had the place surrounded, but he relished the idea of dying in such spectacular fashion, and he didn't mind killing a few policemen in the process. Best to keep a few bullets in the pistol.

Death was a complex textured mystery to CJ. It was strange, but the idea of dying excited him. It was just a question of stepping through to the other side of the shadows, joining those figures in the gloom.

CJ knew the way to the exit, and he knew the layout of his manager's office by the outside door. They might be waiting for him there, protecting the only way out.

He looked upward, letting the water stream down his cheeks like tears. "Damn sprinklers. Fake rain in a fake hallway in a fake hospital."

It made him want to laugh at the steady rush of falling water. It was a pity he hadn't thought of the sprinkler system; it would have been glorious to see the whole farcical illusion burn to the ground. And fire safety was one of his responsibilities, too. Ironic, but you can't think of everything.

Okay, one last turn to the right and he'd be in the little office he shared with the costume department. He moved slowly, beginning to brush past costumes hanging on racks: blue scrubs, plastic aprons, fashionable dresses, pressed suits, skirts with matching belts…

It was so damned dark. Luckily, there was light slanting in from the parking lot standards, but it backlit everything. And there—clearly silhouetted against the glass door—was a cop. CJ could make out the summer jacket. It was the detective's partner. What was the name? Josh-something?

The cop was looking out at the parking lot, standing straight with his hands deep in his pockets. His head was indistinct and at a funny angle, as though he was puzzling over some problem. And that hat? It was a poorly fitting fedora that looked ridiculous. The man had no fashion sense.

Creeping closer, CJ raised Weiss's weapon. He took a second, making sure there wasn't any safety catch. He'd even killed before—his wife in that squalid bedroom in Cleveland. He'd used a knife then, but he'd come prepared with a gun.

CJ was pretty confident that when he pulled the trigger, the cop at the doorway would die. The slug might even shatter the door at this range. After that? Well, most likely a gunfight in the parking lot. Cops had body cams these days.

Maybe his death would get on the news. Nah, those TV wusses would probably blur out his final moments, but they would make a big deal out of the story—not because of him, but because fans of the fucking TV show would be fascinated. It was so exciting, advancing to his Armageddon through the pissing rain towards the bright square of the doorway.

The cop hadn't moved. CJ was so close that he could see… Wait a second.

There was something odd about the black trousers. They didn't hang right on the stocky frame. And the shoes? He couldn't see any shoes, but he was suddenly aware of breathing in the cramped entryway. Any second now, the cop would turn.

CJ decided not to wait. He squeezed the trigger, gently at first, and then, supporting his gun hand the way he'd seen it done on TV, he pressed hard. The gun bucked in his hand three times in rapid succession, and the figure in the doorway spun and toppled.

Almost at the same second, he felt a fierce hand grip his wrist and hard steel jammed against his head.

"Let go of the gun, creep, or we save the public the expense of a trial."

Stunned, CJ let the gun fall and turned.

A stocky plain-clothed policeman was snapping handcuffs on his wrist. He looked dishevelled. He had a soaking wet, white, short-sleeved shirt and no jacket. The shirt was plastered against his rounded body. CJ looked down at the figure on the floor and blinked. He could make out the tripod stand now. It was a tailor's dummy.

"Yeah, just another dummy," Prem Joshi said as he fastened the second cuff. "But you made a hell of a mess of my jacket."

CHAPTER TWENTY-SIX

The EMS medics had expected the bloodied body of a serial killer. Instead, they wound up with an injured cop. They received word they were to take Detective Weiss to Joseph Brant Hospital in Burlington if he was stable, so Weiss found himself on a folded gurney bouncing around in the back of an ambulance. A uniformed first responder shone a light in his eyes and pumped up a pressure cuff, all the while nattering away at him.

"So, do you like the Blue Jays for a wild card spot?"

Weiss liked baseball as a sort of pleasingly aesthetic pastime but had no idea what the question meant. "Do you ask everybody that?"

"Just the ones who probably have concussions and may not be lucid. We could talk about TV if you like. I hear that the place where we picked you up is like a TV studio or something. I had a bad moment back there when we picked you up in that corridor—I thought we were taking you from a hospital to a hospital. You know what I mean?"

It was coming back to Weiss but slowly. He remembered a shower of stars and then…Prem leaning over him, anxious and soaking wet. Prem seemed to be covering him with his jacket, but there was something odd about it—huge, ragged holes right in the middle. He remembered another voice: "Does anyone know how to shut off this fucking rain?"

Weiss had asked about Delana and Barnabé, so he couldn't be too concussed, and Prem had assured him everything was okay. Had his partner said, "You saved Delana" or was that wishful thinking on Weiss's part?

He thought, not for the first time, that he was a terrible field agent. If they'd let him sit at his laptop with his phone handy, he could solve half the crimes in the region, but this business of prancing about with a weapon? It sucked.

He wondered if he had put Prem at risk. Prem's wife—the optician—and their pretty daughter would never forgive him if he had.

The ambulance gave one final swerve, and the back doors burst open. He held on for dear life as two people in scrubs dragged the gurney out, and he felt the clatter of the legs dropping and locking.

Doors. Overhead lights. The squeak of wheels from below. And then more lights pointed directly into his eyes.

A nurse was wiping his face with a pad that came away bloody. The dampness stung, but he could see better now. "Keep him awake. Talk to him."

The medic's voice: "So, about the Blue Jays…"

———

Sometime during the night, he was sat up and given a hard chair in a small examining room. He couldn't remember anyone taking his phone away or removing his earphone, but it was gone, so he was bored.

It was a long night. The first person to come in, at something like three A.M., was an insurance guy from the region who asked a lot of questions about his gun. Before Weiss would answer, he wanted a report on Delana Brazos.

"She's fine. Shaken up but recovering. No lawsuits likely. So, about the gun… You never actually fired at Barnabé?"

"Right."

"You're in pursuit of a serial killer. You have proof of his guilt, and you never ventured a shot?"

"I'm that kinda guy."

"Your suspect wasn't that kinda guy. He pumped three rounds of Halton issue shells into a dressmaker's dummy and another four into an elevator, so there'll be an investigation. Hopefully short."

Weiss slumped even further in his chair and appeared to be washing his face with his hand.

A young Asian doctor came in around four and did the penlight in the eye bit again and asked him how he was feeling.

"My eye socket aches, but it's a dull ache."

"Who is the Premier of Ontario?"

"What? Oh, shit. My mind is fine, okay? Let's not get into politics, and just don't ask me about the damn Blue Jays. Gimme a day to rest and clean up, and I can get back to work."

The next visitor was Detective Antonia Beal, and Weiss's boredom evaporated like a heat haze on the lake.

Toni stepped along the corridor, glancing into the glassed-in rooms in an anxious mix of haste and hesitancy. Weiss wasn't used to seeing her flustered. This was a woman who routinely stared down thugs and traffickers, but when she found his bare white examining room, her head went back, and her eyes closed. "Thank God."

Toni moved to stand in the doorway, suddenly stern, her arms crossed. This was more like it, Weiss thought. This was Toni.

The pose didn't last. She pressed her eyeglasses up her nose and glowered. "Jesus, Eilert." She recoiled at the sight of his bruised and padded brow before swooping in for a hug. "I was up in Halton Hills when I heard. I'm not hurting you, am I?"

He managed to wince in pain and grin simultaneously. "It's worth it."

He was suddenly giddily happy, just because she was here. Toni had two nice, grown kids off at college; but for that, Weiss could imagine that both their lives had been miscues up to this point, and now they were together.

CHAPTER TWENTY-SEVEN

Weiss looked up when he heard a brittle rustling sound. Prem Joshi was slowly peeling back the brown paper from a large muffin, enjoying the moment. He caught Weiss's glance and smiled lovingly at the muffin. "It's called a fruit explosion: cranberries on the outside, gooey jam on the inside."

Weiss nodded. "I'd expect no less of you, Prem." He raised his paper cup. "And thanks for the tea." He couldn't resist adding, "No sugar, no cream. Just tea."

The District Three Station of the Halton Police was situated at Corporal Henshaw Boulevard and Walker's Line. A very short drive up Walker's Line was a plaza with a large Tim Horton's coffee shop. Weiss knew that Joshi appreciated this symmetry, saw it as apt, and took advantage of it at mid-morning break now and then. Joshi's wife worked as an optician in the same plaza, and Joshi would drop by with a coffee for her when he could.

Still admiring the muffin, Joshi took a sip of his own cup—coffee, double-double—before asking, "How's the paperwork going?"

"Fine. Toni and Tom did a thorough search of Barnabé's

house and came up with a load of books: metaphysical stuff, religious incantations, apocryphal tracts. It's pretty obvious his killings were ritualistic. The capper is, he had a coil of human hair in his pocket and a good prosecutor could now tie him to the death of his wife in Cleveland five years ago as well. We may be able to prove that he tracked her down after she left him. One way or another, the prosecution has plenty to send him away for life."

Joshi smiled. "I'm sure your report will be a joy to read. Most cops hate the paperwork. You revel in it. Kind of twisted if you ask me."

"Bringing order to the brutal chaos of life, Prem. That's me."

"You shouldn't even be at work. They would've given you at least a week to recover."

Weiss touched the large white pad taped to his forehead and gave a beatific grin. "I'm fine. It doesn't hurt, and the swelling is going down. Toni has been pressing cold packs on it and cooing over it a lot."

"It's good to have someone to coo. Hard to picture Detective Toni Beal all soft and nurturing, though. I saw her bring down a drunk with an arm lock once."

"Believe me, I've seen her tough side, too. It saved me from falling apart after my wife's suicide. Saved my career, too. Sometimes you get lucky and someone decent comes along and props your life up."

Joshi returned to the muffin, dismantling it slowly, using the flattened paper wrapping as a plate. After he finished it, he swung around to the files open on his own desk. "What about this Amy Cousins business? We've got a break-and-enter charge against the kid, I suppose, but we don't have a motive. And we don't have the suspect in custody."

"You mean we don't have a suspect we could tell anyone about. Nobody wants to hear about a girl missing since the sixties—unless she happens to show up as an elderly woman in her eighties. You're right, though. I'm going to have to write up our visit to Lizzie's place as 'proactive policing' and let it go."

"We might get away with that...unless..."

"Unless the girl keeps showing up on Lizzie's stairs. Right?"

Weiss looked out the office window. A dark blue Halton Police flag was hanging from its pole like a wrung-out rag. Beyond the cool plane of the window, the August heat weighed down on the brown lawns of neighbouring houses and the shimmering road. The inversion hung like a blanket, but the rain had passed.

———

A few minutes after eleven, Weiss's phone diddled a little tune in his jacket pocket. He pulled it out and read the name: Carly Rouhl. He looked around quickly. His partner was out of the office.

"Carly?"

"Hello, Eilert. I'm glad we're past the Ms. Rouhl stage. How's your head?"

"A goose egg and a few stitches. Then there's the bruise on my professional ego." She made a sympathetic moaning sound. Weiss said, "You're cooing. I'm learning to recognize it."

"Am I?" She paused. "Will there be a scar?"

"A small vertical line above my brow, so I'm told. Prem says it will be lost in all my wrinkles. Prem doesn't coo."

"I was hoping we could talk."

Weiss's desk chair creaked noisily. "You hear that? That's me easing back in my chair, and my feet are up—in spirit at least."

"Actually, I thought of asking you to drop by my place. I like the idea of offering you a cup of tea, but the story I have to tell you is nasty. There are enough gloomy memories in my house already. Maybe the park would be better?"

"Not the playground again!"

"The park is right across the street, and this time of year it happens to be full of kids having a great time. Families, picnics, mothers with strollers…" Carly's voice changed; became breathy. "All that life… I think it would help me hold on to my sanity."

Weiss picked up on the worry and looked at the time on his laptop. "I could be there in half an hour."

———

Weiss parked in the lot behind the Art Gallery. Joshi unfolded himself out of the passenger side and looked up at the giant plastic donut perched atop a pole. It marked a lakeside donut shop beside the gallery. The giant donut had colourful sprinkles the size of cinnamon buns all over it.

"I'll be fine here," Joshi said. "The gallery's air conditioned, and it has a coffee machine. This proactive policing has its charms."

Weiss smiled and headed for the rainbow crosswalk to the park. He found Carly on a bench under a tree, her purse spread out as though she were saving a spot for someone. They were a fair distance from the kids' play area this time, but he could hear the gaiety as boys and girls rode swings and self-propelled carousels, climbed on plastic gunwales, and clambered up spider webs made of stout rope.

Carly winced at the sight of his bandage and looked as if she were about to coo, so Weiss quickly said, "How's Evan?" and made ready to sit.

Carly propped the purse on her knee. She was wearing cream slacks and sandals, her summer-bleached hair curling in the heat. She fished a phone out of her bag and looked at the time. "Evan'll be on the air right now. He's talking to Jann Arden today. She gives a good interview."

"Have you seen Lizzie?"

"Lizzie's fine. I told her she wouldn't be seeing any more of Amy."

Weiss turned and looked at her. She wore a welcoming smile, but her brow was tense. "Yes, Amy—Amy Cousins," he said.

Carly blinked at him. "You believe me? You believe I spoke to her?"

"It's all right, Carly. I'm here to listen. I won't judge, and I'll try to keep my mystification light and polite." He mugged an air of aristocratic dignity. "Let's start with why Amy won't be back?"

Carly shrugged. "Because *you* did what she wanted. You stopped the surgeon."

"The surgeon?" Weiss frowned in incomprehension for a moment, but then he said, "You're talking about Barnabé, our serial killer, aren't you? He killed those women on an operating table. Is that what you're getting at?"

"It came to me when I read about you getting hurt at that film studio. It was a hospital set, wasn't it? For a TV show —*Parish*? An OR?"

Weiss nodded. "The media are going crazy about the story because the show is so popular. But what possible connection could there be between a present-day serial killer and Amy Cousins? Poor Amy disappeared when she was nineteen."

"She disappeared because she was murdered by a man named Benjamin Morgan over sixty years ago."

"The Benjamin Morgan who used to own Lizzie's house?"

"That's right. Lizzie's house—which is just across the water from where the old Brant Inn stood. Morgan killed Amy to silence her. It was she who had called him out as a sexual predator in the first place, but no one believed her—'I tried to stop him.' What she wasn't telling us was that she was also the one who had egged him on in the first place, pimping her high school friends to him so he could lure them into his basement and murder them."

"So…what was Amy? A victim, or an accomplice?"

"I think I understand now. She was both. Although 'accomplice' doesn't do her justice. If there's an evil influence here, it was sweet little Amy. She was Morgan's girlfriend because Morgan liked them young and pretty, but she was stronger, more twisted than he was. It was Amy who led him to murder, twice, using her knowledge of his desires to control him."

Carly held Weiss's gaze, her eyes wide, willing him to understand. "Her plan from the beginning was to betray him, act the victim, and get away with what he and she had done as partners. She figured no one would believe that a teenage girl was guilty of murder. But it didn't work. No one believed a teenage girl, period. Especially with no body having been found yet. And Morgan, despite his youth, was a respected bigshot at the Brant Inn when Burlington was an exceedingly small pond. The way the authorities dismissed her only made Amy more confident they could get away with murder. So, she got Morgan to kill again.

"At first, she felt safe. Morgan was under her power, and now that he had killed the first girl, Amy could blackmail Morgan into doing what she wanted. After all, eventually, someone might believe her, but Amy would be fine if they did. She would stick to her story that Morgan was acting alone, and she'd come across as the one who had been telling the truth all along. Morgan would be the obvious killer."

She breathed out, venting her disgust. "But, of course, after they murdered the second girl, Morgan caught on that he had to shut Amy up for good, for his own safety. He wasn't stupid, just weak. He knew she was trying to betray him and put the full blame on him. He finally had the guts to turn on her, and Amy Cousins became victim number three."

"So, Amy really was murdered."

"In the end, it worked for Morgan. He got away with it. No one found Amy's body, and Morgan died in 1997, a respected record producer." Carly squinted at the brightness of the horizon. "My guess is 'poor' Amy Cousins is in the lake. Morgan wouldn't have had to take the bodies far, living on the beach. A few weights, a midnight wade…"

Weiss blinked and said, "Huh." After a second, he added, "And how did you put all this together?"

"It's Evan mostly. He's a great researcher. He came up with this." She opened her bag and pulled out a paperback book. It was a large format edition with a black-and-white photo of a two-story hotel on the cover. Carly held it up for Weiss. There were blue letters across the top of the page reading: "I saw it at the Brant."

"The cover shows the Brant Inn in the late fifties." She opened to an interior page. "And this… This is the Sky Club, an outdoor deck with a band shell where the big names used to perform. It was out back of the Inn overlooking the lake. You could see it easily from the shore near Lizzie's place."

"How does this Morgan guy fit into all this?"

"That part was simple in the end. I'd seen Morgan as a young man, so Evan knew we needed a photo—a photo of the man I saw with Amy. All he did was ask me to look through this book, and sure enough, I spotted Morgan in one of the photos. There he is."

She angled one of the back pages and pointed. "There, see? Standing behind Ella Fitzgerald on her right?" A handsome young man with glasses was grinning out of a black and white past, but his features were clear enough. Carly pointed to the caption beneath the photo. It listed five names, beginning with Ella. "See? Ben Morgan, associate talent coordinator for the Inn."

Carly closed the book and slipped it back into her purse. "Reading about your capture of that Barnabé guy, I was struck by the similarities between the Archer case and Morgan. Morgan used the same bait as your Archer killer.

"Back then, before TV got big, the Brant Inn was mass entertainment. There was a cross-country radio show featuring the biggest bands and singers of the era, and it all happened from Burlington 'on the shores of beautiful Lake Ontario.' And that basement? Lizzie's basement? Morgan played host there to Johnny Mathis, Count Basie, Jayne Mansfield…

"He offered liquor and relaxation to show people, some of whom couldn't get a drink on Sunday, couldn't go to white-only bars and couldn't stay at the best hotels. Did you know Count Basie couldn't even get his car fixed in Burlington because it was a Lincoln Continental and Black people weren't supposed to own Lincolns?

"It must have been an irresistible world for Amy—being part of all that glamour and celebrity—and when Morgan fell for her sweet little sophomore act, she found herself on the fringes of a colourful and slightly seedy circle; lots of pot and hard liquor. Imagine her excitement when she caught on that she was in control of this dapper man. Amy quickly got used to being in control."

Weiss was watching the crowds walking along the chained breakwater, but his eyes were wide. "I'm still not with you. You seem to be saying Amy Cousins somehow managed to show up in Morgan's old house—where Lizzie now lives—just to point us at Barnabé, a modern-day serial killer."

"Poor Eilert. I must drive you crazy with my wild-eyed fantasies." She laughed, but her grin came and went in an instant. "I do have an idea about Amy's appearances. Can't prove anything, of course, but I feel as if I got to know her a bit. My take is that Amy wasn't the type to concern herself with the suffering of others. I don't think she cared about Barnabé killing women. After all, she'd done as much herself using Morgan as a puppet.

"No, I think Amy went to her grave with a lot of guilt on her head. In life, she may have been conflicted, tormented if not by conscience, then by fear of discovery. She had her frenzied excitement, helping Morgan abuse her school friends, but she was living on a knife edge. For someone like her, maybe her own death was a release—a welcome oblivion."

Weiss narrowed his eyes. "I still don't get it. In this story you're telling me, what would bring Amy back? You say she didn't care about Barnabé. What would account for her showing up on Lizzie's stairs?"

Carly steepled her fingers and let her eyelids almost close. "Okay, this is me being my father—the creative writer, the storyteller. And here's the way I figure it: I don't think Amy Cousins cared about the murders you've been investigating, the Archer killings. That wasn't part of her world. Barnabé and his victims had nothing to do with Amy's short time on earth. No, the heart of Amy's life was Lizzie's basement. That's where she goaded Benjamin on, all for the sheer horrific excitement of it all. But yes, Barnabé did bring her back.

"With his operating room and his scalpel, to Amy, Barnabé was the surgeon. That's how he appeared to her, you see. Amy didn't care about stopping the killing of wives and mothers. What was bothering her, what made her rise up Lizzie's stairs..." Carly grimaced at the thought. "I think Barnabé was just...disturbing Amy's sleep, and she wanted it to stop."

His mind racing, Weiss gave a small gasp. It was fiction, but he marvelled at the way Carly could make her story sound plausible and natural. "At Barnabé's place, we found books: ancient incantations and evocations of the dead. Barnabé was a crazy man who thought he could bring his wife back from the dead. In his pocket, we found a braid of hair that connects him to the murder of his wife five years ago."

Carly looked Weiss in the eyes, wondering what he'd make

of what she had said. "I…I know you don't believe in that sort of thing—the incantations and all."

"Barnabé was crazy, Carly. A psychopath." Weiss let his gaze wander to the lake and the slight wash of light that was the horizon. "Those poor women! You know, Barnabé didn't care about them either; Abby, Maria, Alicia, Delana… All he cared about was that *resurrection* nonsense—bringing back his wife: the very first woman he murdered."

Carly nodded slowly. "So, he was weighed down by guilt, too. He must have really loved his wife."

Weiss rubbed his eye, wincing. The brow area was still painful to his touch. "No. I don't call that love. He didn't want his wife back because he loved her. He wanted her back because she was *his,* and she had chosen to leave him. What he did— following her and her lover down to the States and stabbing her to death—was about ownership. That's why he took a length of her hair as a trophy. His so-called attempt at resurrection was about owning her, too."

Irrationally, Weiss found himself hoping Barnabé's wife was at last finally free of him.

———

By unspoken consent, they got up together, Carly gathering her purse and slipping it over a shoulder. They began to walk back towards the crosswalk to the Art Gallery. Carly would just have to cross Maple Avenue and she'd be home.

Before they parted ways, Carly stopped Weiss and studied his face, her eyes darting. "Eilert, what happened in that TV studio, I know you don't put any faith in those old rituals—the books in Barnabé's house. But what Barnabé did in that phony OR is the only link between Amy Cousins and those other dead women, the ones Barnabé killed."

Weiss paused, searching her lovely face, wondering what to

make of Carly's mind. He thought of her peculiar gift of insight, and suddenly he remembered that it was he who had drawn her yet again into his world of human suffering and murder. Was she his lightning rod, or was *he* the one who was an instrument of something he didn't fully understand?

It seemed quite natural for him to give her a quick kiss on the cheek. And then he turned towards the gallery parking lot. Prem would be on his second coffee by now.

Across the street and in sight of the car, Weiss thought about going home to Toni Beal, and a line of poetry ran through his head unbidden: "Time but attends and befriends her."

He understood with a smile that he was re-entering a world where little things mattered—like buying a new car or shaving off his beard. It had been a long, dark journey and a long time since he had last cared so much about living.

———

Later that evening, Evan switched off the TV and stretched. "I'm heading upstairs. Care to come?"

He waggled one eyebrow at Carly in a lascivious way which seemed at odds with his demigod nose and forehead. He should be casting lightning bolts from Olympus, she thought, not leering at her lips. They were Volupté Pink Balm, gloss, number sixteen, so she did sympathize. Carly grinned and peeled aside the woven coverlet which had been draped over her legs. The coverlet had belonged to her mother.

"Go on up," she said. "I'll be right there."

Carly sat for a moment, stroking the nape of her neck, until Evan disappeared on the upstairs landing, and she could hear the bedroom door open. Indy's head came up at the sound so that he was sitting sphinxlike at her feet.

Suddenly, the Lab's head snapped to the left at a similar sound, and he got up to his feet, silent on the carpet. Still seated,

Carly turned to follow his gaze. Indy was peering now at the corridor to her father's office. Her heart skipped a beat, but her shoulders quickly relaxed in relief. Nothing was disturbed; nothing was out of the ordinary.

Carly got up, sleepy and warm. "Okay, Indy, time to turn in."

She stood still for a moment, her eyes following the carpet up to the office door. Then the warmth seemed to bleed from her through her feet.

Almost invisible in the shadows, a tasselled blue bookmark lay on the floor.

THE END

ABOUT THE AUTHOR

Doug Cockell was born in Edinburgh, Scotland and did graduate work in Literature with acclaimed novelist and playwright Robertson Davies at the University of Toronto. Doug has taught Literature, Art, and Media Studies in Oakville and Burlington and was awarded the McLuhan Distinguished Teacher Medal for showing the common visual language shared by illustration, the movies and computers. He has offered courses through The University of Toronto, Brock University, and The Art Gallery of Burlington. In addition to being an author, Doug is an accomplished artist who came to art through his love of the great Twentieth Century illustrators, delighted by their charm and whimsy as well as their skill.

Requiem For Parish is the fourth novel in the Requiem Series. You may wish to check out the first three books in this series if you haven't already done so.

We'd love to know what you thought of *Requiem For Parish*. Please take a few moments to kindly leave a review wherever this book was purchased or email us at dunhillclare@gmail.com to let us know your thoughts. Thank you.